THE DUKE

She was too pretty to hang, but the law said she must. Kitty Devlin had been railroaded for the rope by a cutthroat sheriff and a woman-hating judge. They needed her out of the way . . . and she was going to get it right in her lovely neck.

But the two schemers weren't counting on Duke Parry. The soft-spoken, hard-playing gambler hated a dirty game; Holiday's crooked lawmen were playing with a loaded hand and the Duke was determined to even the odds . . .

THE DUKE

William R. Cox

GUNSMOKE

First published in the UK by New English Library

This hardback edition 2006
by BBC Audiobooks Ltd
by arrangement with
Golden West Literary Agency

ISBN 1 4056 8070 9

British Library Cataloguing in Publication Data available.

Printed and bound in Great Britain by
Antony Rowe Ltd., Chippenham, Wiltshire

Chapter 1

Duke Parry had never been up the Western Trail, but it did not look any better than the remembered dust of the old Chisholm route to Abilene. When he crossed the Washita, he was ready to turn the dun pony westward. He made a dry camp for no reason other than that he was weary and a bit impatient to get on home.

He lay on his back, head propped on the saddle, and looked at the night stars of a June still cool in the Panhandle, and wondered about that word "home."

There was absolutely no reason for him to return to Holiday. The town—west of the trail, south of Dodge City, and barely in Texas—held nothing for him but memories of a boyhood ten years behind. He was twenty-five, he'd seen the elephant, he'd hacked it out for himself, the career, the money which was distributed in several key banks around and about the frontier.

At fifteen he had been orphaned in an epidemic of the fever. The unfrocked Jesuit who had taught the Holiday school had succumbed with his parents and the others. Duke Parry had sold the little store, bought a cutting horse, and hired out to Glover as a trail hand. The romantic life of the cowboy, he had thought, that was for him.

One trip to Abilene had disenchanted him. One look at the color of a faro layout, one glimpse of a pat hand in a table-stakes game had set his course. He had spent most of the store money and a couple of years before he fell in with Br'er Collins and learned the trade right, cheats and all.

Since then it had all been downhill and shady. Even the range clothing he wore was custom-made, though subdued in hue. He ate the best, smoked Havana cigars, walked with the

5

mighty in the western capitals. He lacked not for woman,
wine, or song.

Why did something tug at him always, gently urging him,
taking him back to Holiday?

He had no answer, which annoyed him, for he was a man
always sitting in judgment on himself, a questing man. He
fell asleep.

In repose he seemed younger than when his sharp, dark
eyes were open. He was of average height, stocky in the
shoulders from the early work on the trail. His nose was
longer than good looks required, his mouth wide and mobile
even in dreams. His hair was brown and grew close to his
round skull. He was clean-shaven and square-chinned.

He moved restlessly a few times, then settled into the
blankets, snorting, and was far gone.

In the Holiday House and Bar, business was good, as always. The town lived off the surrounding ranches, where the
red earth was fruitful. Five thousand people lived in or near
the city limits. Kitty Devlin, twenty, snub-nosed, red-
haired, served drinks, wandered among the Saturday night
gamblers, smiled on one and all.

Yet there was a shadow on Kitty Devlin. Every so often
she repaired to the near-deserted dining room to compose
herself. The full-length mirror failed to reassure her this
night. Her green eyes wore shadows, the droop of her small
head was noticeable, her full breasts rose and fell unevenly.
The new dress bought that afternoon seemed not quite right
on her less than ample figure.

Maury Dent came up silently behind her and said, "Is he
getting you down, Kitty—or just letting you down?"

She whirled, staring at the taller, older woman. Maury
was possibly twenty-three or twenty-four. She had been up
and down, from Abilene to Fort Worth. She was presently
waiting on tables in Holiday House, but she was obviously
not a waitress.

Kitty said, "I asked you before, stop cozening me."

"Now that's a New England word, 'cozen,' " smiled Maury
Dent.

"I'm from Maine and I'm proud of it." Kitty tossed her
head and a smile broke through. "Oh, I know you're my
friend. And I know I'm being plumb silly."

"You'd be a lot smarter if you'd pack up and git," said
Maury Dent. "Simon Avidon might have been your first,
but you'll be real unlucky if he's your last."

Red blood crept up to the auburn hair. "I shouldn't have told you."

Maury shrugged; there was a wearied acceptance in her. "You had to tell someone or bust. Better it was me. At your age it's no disgrace to fall for Simon Avidon. So long as it's a lesson learned."

"It's learned. He's going to marry Faith Chittley. He . . . he didn't even tell me. I heard it from Mr. Fitz."

"You still got the knife, Kitty?"

She lifted her skirt, showing the sheathed, sharp stiletto attached to her garter. She said harshly enough, "I'll use it, too, if I have to."

Maury Dent said, "Pray the good God you don't have to. But keep it handy, girl, keep it handy."

She went up the stairs to where she and Kitty had a room on the second floor of the hotel in the rear. Her ankles had been chiseled by a master hand, the set of her head on her rounded shoulders was different from any other woman, Kitty thought. She was a mystery, Maury Dent, and no better than she would be in some other time and place. She was running from something, no question about that, pausing here merely to gain breath before she ran again. More than that, Kitty could not guess.

As for herself, it was horrible to be so young and to have been in love only once and now to be jilted. She made herself go back into the bright, well-kept bar which Fitz Warren ran in his just and kindly manner, with profit but without gouging or taking advantage.

It was not that she minded having been deflowered by Simon Avidon. On this frontier, it might have happened in a much more uncomfortable and indecorous manner. She certainly had enjoyed it, and the succeeding months of the affair had been much more than pleasurable. She had learned, all right, if not exactly what Maury had implied. She had learned what it meant to be a woman with a man.

Fitz Warren, a bit vague, patted her shoulder. He was at least fifty, he was portly, he was a better man than her fisherman father had ever been. He had sailed many seas while her father was tending his lobster pots. He had roamed all over the world, and how and why he had come to Holiday no one knew. He was the sole owner of this hotel and part owner of the Texas Bank. He could have been a power had he chosen.

He preferred to be a good man in a town which did not appreciate him. Nothing fazed him, he moved among them with his small smile, peering out of his faded blue eyes, run-

ning a hand over his balding skull, dealing out his own idea
of justice to one and all.

He said, "Be a good girl and take a few beers over to the
big table. Barkeep's runnin' himself ragged."

She had been neglecting her work, she knew. She moved
swiftly across the room. She would hate to leave Mr. Fitz,
but it was time to go, as Maury had suggested. Her carpetbag, relic of Maine days, was brushed and dusted and ready.
She just hadn't had the heart to begin packing.

It was pleasant in Holiday, except for Simon Avidon.

She picked up the tray of beers, balanced it, sailed among
the tables to where the house poker game was going on. She
was serving the players when he came in.

She could not help seeing him. Even now she felt helpless
at sight of his sleek blond hair, worn rather long, his wide-
spaced gray eyes, the mustache trimmed and virile, the cleft
round chin. He was a tall man, wide in the shoulder, heavy
in hip and legs. He wore the marshal's star on a vest of
embroidered silk; his boots were neat and polished. He was
thirty years old, a native of Savannah, and he was ambitious.

Behind him was Donkey, a shadow, a copy, a man with
the sloping forehead of subspecies. She should have known
better in the first place, Kitty thought, because any man who
would allow Donkey to trail him about could not be good.
The semi-idiot deputy was a horse beater, a molester of
houseflies, a torturer of the unfortunate girls down at Madam
Beesom's.

She took the tray back to the bar. She knew Simon was
looking at her. His bold eyes sought to remind her of other
nights in such a way that she felt hot and cold chills down
her spine. There was no tenderness left in him, just a leering
reminder.

He wanted her out of town, of course. He was going to
marry plain Faith Chittley because her father was mayor,
owned the general store, and had an interest in the bank.
Avidon needed capital, and he could get almost enough from
that source.

But not all that he wanted, Kitty's Maine training told
her. Not enough to swing the land deal. Not enough to make
him the power in the county and state, which was his ultimate
aim. She wondered where he would look for the rest of the
capital.

She saw him slap Mr. Fitz on the back, order drinks. She
saw him lean toward the kindly owner of Holiday House in
that ingratiating way she knew so well.

He won't get far in that direction, she thought. Mr. Fitz

was on to him. All during the affair he had been disapproving. It was his shoulder she had wept upon when the brutal end had come. Mr. Fitz was a quiet man but a bad enemy, even for Simon Avidon.

Yes, she had learned a lot. There was a wonderment in how quickly, under provocation, through fear and disenchantment, a girl could fall out of love. She picked up another tray and went across the room. She had never really taken time to be thoughtful before Simon Avidon had thrown her over. She was, she believed, gaining. Some day she might be a real person, like . . . like Maury Dent?

The trail herd had also crossed the Washita, and was due east of Holiday. There was no chance of an excursion into the town, not under Fairly, a dedicated man. It was a big drive, up from San Antonio, headed for Dodge. The crew was hand-picked, a tough, rough, experienced bunch.

Jack Budington rode in the night. He was twenty-two years old, at that a veteran of the old trail. He owned two hundred head of the cattle he was guarding. He owned a piece of the land down in the county near the Mexican line. He had worked like hell, denying himself Saturday nights in Abliene and Dodge, resoling his boots, patching his saddle. He was known as a responsible, steady-going man.

Yet under the stars of this June night he did not feel solid. The sap stirred in him. He was confusedly aware of yearnings.

He thought of his adobe cabin far to the south, and its cheerlessness and aridity made a sour taste in his mouth. He thought of his life since he had bought his first ten head of cattle; it had been barren, forlorn, lonely.

Oddly, he was not overpoweringly anxious to be a rich rancher. It was only that he had started with nothing, saw clearly that to stay alive a man must work, and he had proved a good worker. Alcohol distressed him; he had no gift at games of chance. He was basically honest and clever enough to divine that the owl-hoot boys were going no place but to destruction. A man usually had little choice in the West—he went good or he went drifting.

At the bank in San Antonio they told him he was the salt of the earth, the backbone of the West to come. He had been neither pleased nor displeased. It was the way things went and there was nothing to be done about it.

Now, sitting hunched in the saddle, he thought of Joe Bounty, his boyhood friend. They had been drawn together by the attraction of opposites. Joe was a boozer, a card player, a fighter. He was an example of—what?

He remembered the time the tinhorn had braced Joe in the gambling house. Joe had outed his six-shooter with speed born of constant practice and downed his man with one shot, a rare occurrence in gun battles Jack had witnessed. That made Joe a bad boy to cross.

When Joe took up his homestead, everyone had predicted dire things for the future. When Joe began swinging a wide loop, the sheriff had made several excursions, trying to put together a necktie party.

Joe proved the best running-iron operator of his time and place. He also learned to skip over the river and grab Mexican steers, a profitable if dangerous pursuit. He built a house and brought in furniture from the East and gave wild parties which lasted days.

One day Joe wandered into town and got drunk and wound up in Miz Carter's house. He laid up with a tall, lean half-Mex half-Irish girl named Marietta O'Riley.

This whore was good-looking, young and wild and happy in her profession. She was picked to become a madam in her own right when her useful days were over by some of the city's expert prognosticators. She made a lot of money, picking pockets and rolling drunks, and she saved it. She had the temper of a cougar and the disposition of a rattler.

Two days after they met, she and Joe were married.

They enlarged the house, had a baby, and were the happiest pair of people Jack Budington knew.

It just depended, he thought wistfully, on how the cards were stacked. His own dull, laborious way was certain, but it wasn't any fun.

Maybe he was lacking in something, he thought. Maybe he wasn't built to have fun. Maybe he would never see a woman that could mean as much to him as Marietta did to Joe.

It came down to that. If a man didn't like booze or cards, there was only womankind left. He blinked at the stars, and the stars blinked back at him. There was no answer in the sky.

The answer, he knew in his plodding, honest way, was inside the man himself. He had brains enough, more than Joe, maybe not more than Marietta, but certainly more than Joe. He did not have Joe's capacity for restless change, Joe's daring and his flair for the dramatic.

What could he do? He knew the answer. He could sell his cattle in Dodge, bring back the money, buy more cattle, improve the breed with Herefords, and become one of the richest bachelors in Texas. What was there to prevent him?

He shook his head, thinking of Joe. The whores Jack climbed in his necessary excursions into houses were never like Marietta. Even when he was desperate, they were barely palatable.

He cut over to a straying muley, nudged it back into the herd. He relapsed into somnolence, pushing his thoughts away from women.

Someday, maybe, when the time came, he would know what to do. Meantime he was Jack Budington, a coming young rancher respected by everyone but himself.

Chapter 2

DUKE PARRY hauled into Holiday on Sunday evening, in the cool. He looked for change, found very little. The town had always been quiet, satisfied in its modest prosperity, content with agricultural sufficiency, with the good grass for its stock, like taking in its own wash, as the Chinese made it some places in California, people said. The church bell was ringing, and Duke remembered Father Hal, who winced—despite his apostasy—at sound of that Unitarian tolling.

There had never been a real boom in Holiday. There was no mining, the railroad was not headed this way. The slow growth of homebred farming was aided by a small sawmill out where a tributary of the Red River meandered down from the north into this valley, between the old cattle trail and the new.

There was one main street, Holiday Avenue, crossed at intervals by numbered streets which ran east and west. On the side streets running parallel to Holiday Avenue, named for trees, there were houses of adobe, clapboard, even one or two of brick brought in at great expense. There were small lawns and some flowers sheltered from the Texas sun by various devices. It was an odd sort of town for this country. Maybe that was why Duke came back. There really was no place he knew like Holiday.

The store his father had owned had grown larger, but that was to be expected. The name over it meant nothing to him, "Chittley," and he knew there would be new people by the number of houses banked on the back streets. He saw a man strolling along, a man with clothing cut better than those who had lived in the town in his day. He tied up at the rack in front of Holiday House and Bar, and the man came closer, peering in the uncertain light, a bit stooped, his hands loose and easy near his holstered guns; here was a new and amazing addition to Holiday life, indeed.

The Duke's heels hit the board walk, and he paused. He wore no cartridge belt for reasons of pride. It disturbed the cut of his tailor-made clothes. The man had no such delicacy, and then Duke saw the badge on his fancy vest.

Simon Avidon said, "Howdy, mister."

"Good evening," said Duke. "You a stranger here, mister?" He unslung his rifle and held it under his arm.

Avidon shook his blond head. "I'm supposed to ask that question."

"Try answering it." The Duke was inches shorter, but he seemed big enough, standing there, staring at the marshal.

Avidon said, "Maybe we ought to go inside and start over in the light."

"You think so?"

"I'm the town law." The voice drawled, slurring syllables all over the place. "I got a right, sir."

Duke hesitated. He neither trusted nor liked this man on sight, even in the half-light. Yet he wanted no trouble, and he could be wrong. Once or twice he had been wrong about a man he had just met up with.

He finally said, "I'll just take my truck inside. Meet me in the bar."

Avidon nodded. He stood and watched the stocky man walk across the boards, up the steps, and into the hotel lobby. He could hear bells ringing. He, too, was intuitive. He had been five years in Holiday without losing a trick but without gaining as quickly as he wanted. He could not afford a mistake. He had to take it easy, but the bells seldom failed him.

There was trouble in this quiet, unafraid stranger, unless he could be enlisted . . . or quickly squelched.

Inside the hotel, Duke was signing the book under the eye of a red-haired, green-eyed girl. He looked at her appraisingly, neither approving nor criticizing, just looking. She bridled and handed him a key on a wooden tab. He fingered the worn tab and remembered that he had stayed in the same room for a few nights after the funeral of his parents, and this led him to ask, "Where's Fitz?"

"If you knew Mr. Fitz, you'd know he's at church."

"Forgot about church," he admitted. He looked at her again. "Down East, huh? Sharp tongue."

"None of your business."

"Quite right, ma'am." He touched the roll brim of his forty-dollar hat. "No offense."

She softened. "I'm Kitty Devlin. I work here."

"Nice to make your acquaintance. I used to live here."

"Figured that. You knowing Mr. Fitz. Been away long?"

"Ten years. Don't sound like a lot when you say it fast."

She sighed, and shadows returned to her pert countenance. "Ten years ago I was back home, handling Maine lobsters for my mean old father. In June it was beginning to warm up and I got to swim. Ever try and keep clean with salt water?"

"California way," he nodded. "Don't think much of it."

He picked up his war bag and his rifle and started for the stairs. Then he stopped, turned back, and said, "You might let Fitz know I'm here when he gets back."

She returned his gaze with cool frankness. "Reckon he'll know it right soon, Mr. Parry. You being that kind of man."

He went on up to Number Nine, a good, big room, clean and without crawling life. He sat for a moment or two on the edge of the bed, getting the feel of home.

It was as near as he would ever get, he supposed. The death of his parents had thrown him into a spin. Mr. Fitz had been his bulwark, had tried to get him to stay, had offered him guardianship. Coming out of the whirl of his youthful emotions, however, Duke had only thought of escape from painful memories.

No boy of fifteen with big dreams fostered by a romantic mother who hated storekeeping would have remained in Holiday. He knew that now. His father had been a kindly, bearded, distant man, short and wide and powerful. His mother, almost as tall as her husband, willowy, lovely, was of a different strain. She had been a Fairfax, and Duke Parry was out of that Virginia breed.

No, he had to go. . . . He washed in the white, heavy basin. He hung up his clothing with great care, decided to dab-clean his body, got out his private soap and used a jerry cloth he had from a sailor, called a sweat rag, a handy thing for a man whose pursuit of cleanliness amounted to a peculiarity in his day and age.

He got out a white shirt, a black alpaca jacket, and dark drill trousers. He took his pistol from the war bag and cleaned it, spinning the cylinders.

It was a peculiar weapon, if only because of its short barrel. It was a .38 Caliber Colt's. It was squat and ugly. He stood up, slipped it out of sight.

The hang of it was perfect. It fitted snugly into a leather-lined pocket of his trousers. Gun and pocket were built for each other like hand and glove. He made sure of it by snapping the weapon out with a careless flip of his right wrist—the motion was much faster than a snake striking.

He adjusted the jacket on his rather bulky shoulders and tried the cut-away line of the front of it from long habit, making sure a flick of his finger would clear the gun butt. He faced himself in the glass, sorrowed that he was not taller and handsomer, and went out into the hall.

He thought about the man with the star, knowing that the marshal would be expecting him to come through from the lobby into the bar. He liked always to disappoint those who did not enchant him, so he turned for the back stairs which he remembered well. He was going past the last door in the hall, with the light of the wall lamp behind him, when the portal opened and a woman stepped into his path.

Each stopped dead, startled. The light fell on the woman's face, and Duke said softly, "Well, Maury. Thought you'd gone on before now."

"Jesus in Heaven!" She seized his arm, reopened the door, dragged him into the room. "You never said you were coming this way."

The room was smaller than Number Nine. It was warm and neat, and she still used that elusive scent which was like the odor of wildflowers. There was only one chair. She sat on the bed, her feet together. She was wearing a soft dress of quiet gray and slippers. Her ankles were the best part of her, he had always thought, at least when she was dressed; her ankles and the way she carried herself.

She said, "It saved me, coming here. But you knew that when you sent me from Dodge."

"Nobody ever rightly knows." He thought she looked weary in spite of the surcease of living these months in Holiday.

"You do. Damn you, Duke, you know too much." She smiled. Her teeth were remarkably good. She had always been healthier than her way of life seemed to allow.

"People got different ways," he said. "Way I figure, it doesn't make a lot of difference about what they do. It's the way they go that proves what they are, the direction they head into."

She winced. "Sure. I was going out."

"Overdose of laudanum." He grinned, which made him look years less than his age. "How many while you were in Dodge?"

"Dozen, fifteen among the girls. Maybe six broken-down eastern soft boys."

"How many of the girls did it on purpose?"

"I don't know. Nobody'll ever know. They take to it because they can't stand things. It's easy to buy, it cures a hangover. Then you get dreams. When does the dreaming stop and the wish to die begin?"

"Watch yourself," he cautioned. "You're beginning to talk like a lady again."

She flushed. She was touchy only on that point. The Jesuit had implanted in Duke the sure knowledge and acceptance of English usage. Maury Dent—or whatever was her real name—had been educated at some expense, Duke was well aware. It was her business whether or not she chose to conceal the fact. She repeated, "You know too damn much."

"You didn't bring the laudanum bottle with you, I know that."

"Didn't I, though?" She fished around on a shelf above the bed. She showed him the blue vial. "I brought it just to prove something to myself."

"Yes. That's good."

"I've stayed here because there's no place else to go. No reason, that is, for going elsewhere." She stared at him. There was a glow on her face that had been building since she met him in the hall. "Maybe I was waiting for you, Duke. Maybe you're going to point the way."

"We went through all that in Dodge."

The glow died. "Yes. You never minced any words."

His voice was even. "Maury, you're a hell of a woman. Once on the trail, there's nobody can beat you. But you know well enough what your trouble is."

"Maybe I'm different. Maybe I've changed. Isn't it possible that I could change?"

"Anything is more'n possible, with you."

"'I've been waiting on tables. A redhead named Kitty Devlin is the bar hostess or whatever you want to call a decent enough bargirl. I've been carrying trays and washing dishes. Look!" She spread out her hands. They were reddened and slightly cracked, but a few weeks of rest would cure them and restore them. They were another good feature, her lady's hands, long-fingered, agile, strong, talented on the keys of a honky-tonk piano.

"You got a stake?" He didn't want to get into an argument with her. Sometimes she could whip him with words.

"I've got your money and more." She hesitated. "I'd rather pay you back some other time, Duke, if it's all right. You said any time."

"Maury, if you need more, if you got an idea that needs backing, I'm your man."

She looked at him hungrily. "I wish you were my man, you gambling damfool."

"Wouldn't want to cut into the local trade." He laughed, trying to put condescension in his voice. She came off the bed like a wounded virgin.

She stormed, "Not a single man since Dodge. Not one, you hear, Duke Parry? Goddam you, don't treat me like a worn-out old whore you saved from the laudanum bottle. Don't hand me your stinking charity, your smug, fat little hand to kiss. I'll stick it up you so far you'll have the bends for a month of foul Saturdays, you tinhorn bastard."

He rose and opened his arms wide, grinning widely. "Maury! You're all right! You're my wild and woolly doll, cut out of a sheepherder's whiskers."

She sat down again, then looked up. There were tears in her fine eyes. "You sonofabitch!"

"Had to find out somehow. You talk and talk but you got the white woman's forked tongue," he said. "You're a dis-honest dame and you know it."

"I was. Maybe I'm getting better. I'm not cured." She spoke slowly. "Of course I'm not cured. I've got a bitterness through my soul that maybe can't be erased. If I could pray . . . but hell, if I could pray I wouldn't be me. I do think of you Duke. You're the only man that's meant anything to me since . . ." She bit it off. No one knew Maury's story, no one ever would.

He said, awkwardly for him, "Why, Maury, I reckon I think about you. I mean, like I say, you're a hiyu damn woman."

"The best you ever had?" She smiled without guile or rancor. "You always said that, anyway."

"The best I ever had." He took her work-maculated hand. "I'll be around a little while. Right now I've got to see the lawman. He's plumb nosey."

The soft expression left her, and she became alert, sharp-eyed. She spoke crisply, economically. "Simon Avidon. The snake of Holiday. The prime bastard. Don't give him a damn quarter of an inch, Duke."

"Why, Maury, I wouldn't give that hombre the sweat off my elbow."

"No, I mean it, Duke. This is a nice town. Unfortunately, the mayor is a jackass, the good citizens are too fat, and Avidon's got them fooled."

"Fitz?"

"No, but Mr. Fitz grows soft with the years. The little redhead, Kitty—you saw her at the desk?"

"Not my kind," grinned Duke.

"She was Avidon's kind. He practically raped the kid. She liked it, and it went on for sometime before I got here.

Then he decided to amalgamate with Mayor Chittley. So he bounced Kitty and proposed to Faith, a poor, plain, dumb girl. Now he's on the make for Mr. Fitz. Avidon's a growing lad. Growing like a wart on the face of Holiday."

"On marshal's pay?"

"I told you he was smart. He's got the biggest ranch in the valley. He owns houses and lots in the city. He owns the Aces Up Saloon, although he denies that. Playing marshal merely gets him the law on his side. Come to life, Duke. This is a dangerous, smart man."

"I figured him quick, but not good enough," said Duke. "Thanks, Maury. You always had the brains."

"And never used them," she said. "Watch Avidon. This is your town. He's out to take it over."

Duke shook his head. "Maury, you know me better'n that. If this city is dumb enough to let him take it over, that's what this city deserves. I fight no man's battles but my own."

She sighed and nodded. "Which is why you're alive and why I'm alive. O.K., Duke. See you later."

She was able to draw a mantle around herself, diminishing the flame of her personality until it barely glimmered. He had noted this in Dodge, which was one of the elements that had interested him in her. The other things he had better not remember at this moment, he knew, with the bed so close behind her magnificent body.

"I'll be around . . . if your bad boy don't get me quick."

He went down the back stairs. He was going through the rear door when he felt, rather than saw, a menacing figure in the shadows, saw an arm lifted.

He took the pistol out of his pocket in that twinkling, magic manner of his, ducked, and came up swinging. The gun, held tight in his hand, made the sound of a wooden stick knocking a melon open.

The body of the man sagged, went down. For a moment Duke thought it was Avidon himself, angry at being kept waiting, outthinking his man and attempting direct action. Then he lit a lucifer and saw the sloping forehead, the dimmed features, and knew it was only a faint copy of Avidon.

He saw the deputy's star. He chuckled to himself. Avidon was clever, at that. Put a watchdog on the only other entry to the bar, make excuses about any accident that might happen. The marshal took no chances at all. Any man who didn't bow down and answer questions had to be taught a lesson.

He got hold of the fallen deputy's collar and began dragging him toward the door to the barroom. The time for guile had ended when he was attacked. It was now the occasion upon which Avidon must fish or cut bait.

Chapter 3

SIMON AVIDON leaned negligently on the bar. Church services were about over, and Fitz would be returning to the Holiday House. It wasn't time for Simon to go the churchly way; that would come later, after he was married at the altar. Everything in its place, he thought.

He could manage an easy smile. He hoped it was easy, because he was worried about the new man in town and he could not afford to show it. He wished devoutly that he needn't harbor these quondam fears.

They were part of his life. Ever since his mammy in Savannah had crooned the bogey stories about the Big Swamp and the Fool Killer and some fairly horrible ghost tales from her near-African background, he had been ridden by skittish fears. Not because of Mammy, he told himself; it's in some men and maybe it's good for me. Forewarned is forearmed.

He had a short way to go, now, he felt. Fitz Warren would come around. They would pool their interests, remodel the Aces Up and make it the cowboy hangout, share the water which Simon needed and was on Fitz's property adjoining his ranch. Between them they could run things real good.

Between them they could minimize Chittley's superior financial position. It was bad enough to marry an ugly girl for money without having her father lord it over him. The main thing was to move in on the bank, and Fitz could do that for him because Fitz was a founder of the bank.

He had been courting Fitz for a long time, now. The business with Kitty had been a setback, no question of it. He didn't blame himself; he never could see where it was wrong to take a woman who was available. Nothing in his ancestry or training had pointed a different way of life. Still, Fitz had disapproved, had been sore at him.

Well, that was over. The slate was clean. Good-natured, kindly old Fitz would forgive and forget. A little more time and all would be well. Easy does it, he cautioned himself, sipping at his whiskey. Slow and easy, Simon, and you'll own this town lock, stock, and barrel before you're Fitz's age. There'll be elections, a new mayor. Sometime or other Austin won't seem so far away. . . .

As for Faith, well, a busy man took trips. Might run up to Dodge, over to Kaycee. Even Chicago—Simon had never been to Chicago. There were plenty lovely women in the big cities. What Faith didn't know would never hurt her.

He was distracted by a thumping noise in the back, where he had stationed Donkey for no good reason other than that he hated to be taken by surprise. He forced himself to remain passive, only turned when the unusual bumping and dragging noise demanded his attention.

He turned and saw the new man dragging Donkey by the collar through the rear door into the bar. Donkey's heels made a curious sound as though he were dancing light-footed. The stocky stranger hauled him into the light, looked soberly down at him, peered at Simon Avidon.

"Fella here jumped me," said he. He leaned close, looked up with wide eyes. "Why, Marshal! He's wearin' a star!"

"That's my deputy, Donkey Hart. You've made a mistake."

"Not me. I didn't make any mistake." The man gestured at Donkey. "He made a mistake. Look at him if you don't believe me. Got a lump on his skull."

Simon said, "I'm afraid you're under arrest, sir, until Donkey comes to."

"That's interesting." The man moved to the bar, gestured. Holy Jim, the bartender, grinned. The best bottle came out.

Holy Jim said, "Welcome back, Duke. Been a right long time."

The front door opened, and the church people came in, Fitz and Mayor Chittley and some other soberly dressed men of substance. Fitz came directly to Duke, stared at him, then threw his arms about the wide shoulders.

"Duke, these old eyes ain't seen such a sight since the last calvin' of Old Bess."

"Had to come home to make sure you were behavin'."

Other old-timers crowded around. On the floor, Donkey shook his head, mumbled something, started to arise. Simon Avidon went close to him, jerked him erect. Under cover of the hullabaloo around Duke he whispered, "You were wrong,

you dam' fool. You thought it was a thief. You were wrong,
see?"

"He's chain lightnin'," whimpered Donkey. "He moves too
quick. He's got a rock in his hand."

"You've got one inside your head. Now, pay attention.
You—were—wrong. You apologize to him."

Donkey felt the lump over his ear. His cloudy eyes began
to clear. He wiped them once with a bandanna, then blinked
at Duke. He turned to Simon Avidon.

"Hell, Marshal, that's Duke Parry. Knew him when he was
a button. Hell, ain't you never heard of Duke Parry?"

He had heard of Duke Parry. For a moment a clot of envy
choked him. The town hero, the boy who made good in the
big trail towns; he had heard enough about him. The fast
gun—he knew now why there was no holster, no cartridge
belt. He took note of the fashionable clothing, of finest ma-
terial, cut by the best tailors of Denver. He dropped his gaze
to the soft, low-heeled, handmade boots.

He was himself in another moment. Maybe the bell had
been tolling within him because good fortune had arrived in
the guise of Duke. He shoved forward, making himself believe that. He stuck out his hand, looming over the smaller
man, his voice hearty, loaded with Savannah charm.

"You were *so* right, Duke. A bad mistake. Donkey thought
you were a thief we were expectin'. Please accept my humble
apologies."

It didn't seem as though Duke was looking up at him. It
was disconcerting, but Duke seemed to be staring him straight
in the eye. The inner bell gave a last haunting tinkle.

"Why, that's all right. Donkey never did have good sense."

"He's the only deputy I have. Holiday's a quiet town.
Don't need much law."

"Sure, that's right." Duke turned to Fitz. "Reckon Judge
Shelley's still presidin', huh? Still the shinin' legal light of
Holiday County?"

Fitz's easy grin tightened. "The jedge is still functionin'
on all fronts."

"Too bad."

They all turned to the bar. It would be a gay homecoming,
Simon Avidon saw. He might as well join in. There was nothing else to do. He would have to get to the judge as soon as
feasible. It was bad luck, he knew now. Duke's reference to
Shelley could not be misunderstood. It was bad luck all
around, and the homecomer might also affect the projected
deal with Fitz. The little fears began racing about inside his

head again. It was all he could do to maintain the toothy smile which was his stock in trade.

He got away as soon as he could. The judge would be in his office on Holiday Street, returned from church, giving full attention to Blackstone. The Judge did not drink whisky nor use bad language; he was a student. The judge did not care for women, either, Simon Avidon thought, walking down the deserted avenue. He preferred books. Yet Shelley wasn't a day over forty.

Every man has a quirk or two. There wasn't anything wrong with Royball Shelley. He was also a Southerner, an Alabaman. He was an educated gentleman. He was Simon's greatest ally, and the marshal's job had proved a great conjunction for them. The law officer was supposed to confer often with the magistrate. Between them, Simon and Royball Shelley were all the law in Holiday.

He quickened his step, thinking now how to use this important fact to his advantage. His plans were narrowing down, and he had to consider what would happen if Fitz did not fall in with his ideas.

Sometimes he was amazed at the convolutions of his brain. Without bidding, it seemed, ideas appeared, like pictures reeling through his mind. The judge understood and appreciated this. He turned in at the judge's office.

Royball Shelley looked up from the thick, calf-bound volume. His face was hatchet-thin. His eyes were deep-set beneath overhanging, heavy brows. His coloring was pallid, with a delicate flush in the hollows of his cheeks. He wore funereal black, set off by a white stock tightly wound around his long neck. He was forty but appeared to be fifty.

"Good evening, Simon. I understand that you have met the prodigal."

Avidon sat down heavily. The office was square as a box, its walls lined with books. It was immaculate, the judge's desk was swept clean. There was a hospital air about the room, as though everything here was antiseptic.

"How you hear things so fast beats the fool out of me."

"The law is omnipotent."

"That's what I like to hear," murmured Simon Avidon, "on account of we are the law."

"I remember Parry." The sunken eyes burned. "He refused to allow me to handle his parents' estate. A headstrong, virile youth with false dreams in his head. His mother was a weak, foolish woman. Far too much ardor. The father was a fool about her. The boy was christened 'Duke' through some foolishness of the mother. She was a Fairfax, there was nobility

far back. Some younger son, I believe, forced to emigrate to
Virginia, founded the family."

"What size boots does he wear?" The exactitude of the
judge's information sometimes irked Simon.

"Seven. He has small feet, large hands, supple and quick.
He has killed two men, both of whom asked for trouble. He
has buffaloed many that he might have killed with impunity.
He is a friend of Bat Masterson and Wyatt Earp. He has
money in seven banks. He owns a portion of the Long Branch
Saloon in Dodge City and has interests elsewhere, all solid."

Admiration banished the sarcasm uppermost in Simon's
thought. "Anything else?"

"He is dangerous. He is one who walks the land tall because the West is raw and lawless. In the future he will either
turn to legitimate enterprises or go underground with a
gambling enterprise. At present he is a man to deal with in
all caution."

"I surmised that myself."

The judge permitted himself a smile. It had amazing
warmth for the man across the desk. "You are no fool,
Simon. You have an agile imagination. If you would eschew
liquor and cease being a fool about women, you could go
far in this uncertain, fumbling world of the frontier."

"I mean to go far, Judge. With your help."

The thin man made a steeple of his long, slender fingers.
He leaned back, relaxing, looking up at the ceiling. "Yes.
There is no limit if a strong mind is applied to the problems
of a simple civilization. We are dealing with inferior intelli-
gences, Simon. The strongest methods can be undertaken so
long as the law is properly administered."

"I'm going to brace Fitz soon, any time now. He'll be
softened up by this Duke's return. Maybe he'll want to retire, sell out what I need."

"He will never sell to you. He will never go in with you.
Especially now, with Duke Parry to bolster him."

Simon Avidon was stunned. Never before had the judge
been so emphatic in denying him. He gasped, "How do you
know?"

"I've always known." The dry voice was calm. "I have
permitted you to go ahead because it was necessary for your
over-all plan to take form. The goal must be firmly in mind
before the race begins."

"But Judge, it all depends on Fitz. He holds the key."

"Quite right."

"Then what?"

"You will find means to go onward. Even now your mind

is turning over alternatives. You have rid yourself of that low woman. You have ingratiated yourself with the mayor." The dry voice hesitated, then went on. "You will marry the local heiress. Oh, you'll find a way, Simon. I have utmost confidence in you."

He reopened the book. It was a dismissal. At moments like this Simon felt lost, adrift.

"I wish . . . I wish you could hint at some way to go."

"You must try Fitz Warren. It's proper to try him. How else can you know that I am correct?" The judge turned a leaf, found his place, smiled again.

Simon got up. He felt like a small boy being excused by teacher.

"Well, maybe we'll talk about it later."

"After you've broached the subject to Fitz."

At the door Simon paused, looked back. The judge was already buried in Blackstone. There was nothing to do but go out into the street. He had to make a duty call upon Faith.

His heels hit too hard on the boards. His mind was unfolding. The picture was black, then shadowy with grays. Sweat broke out on him. Plan and counterplan took over, unbidden.

"In for a penny, in for a pound." That was an old saw. It was true, though, and he was in for a lot more than a penny.

"Strong methods," the judge had said. Funny thing about the judge, he was a stickler for the law, but he had a way of suggesting a course outside the law of the frontier. He had utter contempt for his contemporaries.

Lots of funny things about the judge, but Simon Avidon could depend on him—he knew that as well as he knew his name. Just give the old boy something to hang on a paragraph from his books, or even something he could make seem like a legal way to go, and he would back Simon to hell and gone.

He wiped the sweat from his face. One step at a time, be ready for all the twists and turns, and look out for Duke Parry—that was the way the road led.

Duke Parry was conscious that he had been drinking too much, a rare happenstance, and that he was talking too much, which was even rarer. Home was doing strange things to him. Fitz's worn, kindly countenance, the attention of the old-timers and a few young cowhands and even hang-mouthed Donkey had opened up a faucet.

"It wasn't like the Texans say," he went on. "Driskill and

Morrison and the boys were on the prod. Wyatt had buffaloed them both in the past. They needed it, take my word. Wyatt is a Yankee, all right, but he's a lawman who walks straight."

"No damyankee can walk straight," said a lanky young waddy.

Duke looked him in the eye. "Wyatt and Bat are friends of mine."

Every eye was on the boy, who dropped his head and mumbled an apology.

Duke said, "I was down the street, havin' supper. Charlie Bassett was out chasin' the Cheyenne and not carin' to find 'em, knowing old Dull Knife. They caught Wyatt in front of the Long Branch—Driskill, Morrison, and maybe a couple dozen trailhands."

He paused, remembering that night in Dodge. "You got to remember how it is. You've been up the trail, a lot of you. The lawmen are your enemies. Now, I never wore a badge and never would, but I couldn't see fightin' lawmen for a bucket full of beans. Sure, a lot of 'em are Yankees. But we go up to their towns. They don't come down here after us."

Fitz said, "In my time we was thirsty in Abilene. We was bottled up and randy and had money in our pockets. Mostly we was drunk."

"Right after the war, I made the Shawnee Trail to St. Louis," said Poley Meyer. "They didn't fool with us in St. Louis. They put us under the jail."

"You didn't need it?"

"We needed it. But you can't tell that to a young fella bustin' out all over from ridin' with ugly men and dumb critters for them months."

"Driskill and Morrison weren't exactly boys," said Duke. "They had young 'uns behind 'em when they cornered Wyatt that night. They had twenty-five, twenty-six guns. Wyatt was alone. He just stood there, knowing his time must be up. He never winked at 'em when they cursed him. He was fig-urin' how many he could down. I know that skinny devil."

"Is it true what they say about him, that he's plumb cold?" asked Fitz.

"Cool, sure. I wouldn't say cold. Smart, a good gambler. Gun-quick. If Driskill and the others hadn't been drunk, they might have thought about that, but there were so many of them, and each one thought it wouldn't be *him* that got it. Like a battle."

He remembered his time riding dispatches and the brief episodes with the Indians. Nobody believed an arrow or a

bullet had his name on it, or there wouldn't be war, he supposed.

He said, "Inside the Long Branch, Cock-eye Frank Loving
was dealin' and a mean-looking lunger was buckin' him and
winning." He paused, grinned. "The lunger spells his name
with two l's, so nobody will ever think our town was named
for him."

"Doc Holliday," said Soapy Simms, a ranch foreman. "I
know that sonofabitch of a thief. *And* his woman, the bitch."

"You know him," said Duke. "Well, that's sort of the
point of the whole story. Doc heard them cursing Wyatt. He
wasn't any particular friend of Wyatt then. Just sort
of thought Earp was a right kind of man, I reckon. Nobody'll ever know why he did it."

"Probably figured to steal a poke," muttered Simms.

"You call it," said Duke. "I was comin' from the China-
man's when I heard the finish. Doc come roarin' out of the
Long Branch with two guns in his hands. He cursed them.
Men, I tell you, he called Morrison and Driskill to judgment.
Then Wyatt got out his guns. Then things got awful quiet. I
was runnin' when the shot was fired. I saw the cowboy go
down. I saw Wyatt lay that Buntline alongside a head. And
I saw that mob treed."

"Holliday killed another man," said Simms. "He would."

Duke shook his head. "Hit him in the shoulder. Doc was
some put out about it. Blamed the bad light. Again—that
ain't the point. It was a thing of one man racked up to die.
Then another man butts in. Then the two of them stand off
two dozen tough, fightin' Texans. I'm not drawin' big con-
clusions. I just want to say one thing: I'm real glad I was
around to know this thing happened and how it happened.
It was an experience, gents, that I would not have missed."

The whiskey was dying. He didn't know why he had bothered to tell the story, except that someone had asked about
Bat and Wyatt. He could have told any number of funny
stories about Masterson, who was a gay blade closer to the
hearts of his audience. He could have told the story of the
baby contest. He could have told how Cock-eye got killed
in a ridiculous gun battle with a boy who couldn't hit a bull
in the tail with a shovel.

Well, the hell with it. He stood up, found that his balance
was good. He waved good night and somehow found himself
going for the back stairs. He went up slowly. The booze was
a banked fire now, but the burning was there. When he came
to the small corner room, he hesitated.

Maury opened the door. She looked at him, then said, "I got the girl in with me. Go to bed, Duke."

He obediently went to Number Nine. His hand was steady with the key. He unlocked the door, stepped to one side, toed it open. He had the pistol in his hand from long habit. He waited a moment, then slid inside the room.

There would be trouble, someday, because Simon Avidon was built that way. A few words with Fitz had corroborated everything told him by Maury. Unless he drifted on, there would be something going. It wasn't the kind of trouble he cared about. He believed every man should look out for himself, and that all the men of a town were better able to do this than any individual.

He took off his hat, rolled the brim, and placed it carefully upon a shelf. He had long since abandoned the cowboy method of undressing from bottom to top. He folded the clean shirt into a drawer of the low, marble-topped dresser.

The boots came hard, but he managed them. He slid out of his trousers and hung them on a peg by the back of the belt. He knew some dudes who used small stovepipes to maintain the creaseless rotundity of pants legs but he liked his own way, tugging the corners, letting them hang loose.

He took off the cotton underwear, wondering why men wore the drawers ankle length in summertime. He took the basin to the window and ran the dirty water down sloping eaves to the wooden gutter which carried it to the drainpipe.

There was enough water left in the pitcher to wash again. The soap smelled clean and sharp. The whiskey was just right now; he had refrained from one over the dozen it took to get him down.

He blew out the lamp and lay on the bed. He thought about Dodge City and the story he had told. He thought he knew now why he had related it.

Wyatt and Tighlman and Bassett were different from Bat and Duke Parry. They believed in exercising authority under the law. They were born badge-wearers.

Bat was elected sheriff by a fluke. He liked to perform, he liked to show his mettle. He was pretty good, too. He made them pay attention. But in his heart Bat was a gambler and a fun-lover. He wasn't a very good gambler, but he was a whale of a love-maker and party man.

Duke wasn't so careless as Bat. He took care of his winnings and he seldom lost. He invested and expected to make a profit. He had fun, sure, and he had women when the time was right. But his father's blood, he now saw, prevented him from roistering down the lane.

He thought about Maury down the hall, but that wasn't the way to sleep, so he ran over the faro layout, making bets, then playing dealer and turning cards and making the payoffs and collections. This was guaranteed to tire the mind and bring on slumber. It worked, as always.

Jack Budington turned in his blankets, unable to drop off, unwilling to get up. Fairly saw him and came over, a big man with brawny arms, hands like steel hooks, and a mind which usually kept to one track: bring the herd through.

"You all right, Jack?"

"Sure, I'm all right."

"Been off your feed. Better take some sulphur and molasses."

"What the hell you think I am, a kid?"

"I don't care what you are. I don't want no sick man holdin' up the drive."

"Who's sick? You lost your cotton-pickin' apples, Fairly?"

The trail boss hunkered down reflectively, looking at the young man. "Well, I dunno, Jack. Seems like you never snarled and snorted like you're doin' right this minute."

Jack regained his temper with effort. "Reckon that wasn't right, Fairly. Only I ain't sick."

"You got money troubles?"

"Nope."

"You got the old ral?"

"Hell, no!"

Fairly split his granite face in a grin. "Never had it . . . and hope you never get it again, huh?"

"The cowboy's curse." Jack's good humor was restored.

"No worse'n a cold in the head. Only I'd rather have double gallopin' consumption." He tipped back his sombrero. "Howsomever. . . . what's the gal's name?"

"I told you I never . . ."

"Didn't mean that. Mean the one you're moonin' over."

The boss driver had always been more than friendly. Jack relaxed and stared up at the stars. "No pertic'lar gal."

"I see. Just in gen'ral, huh? The cabin gettin' lonely on winter nights?"

"You could say so."

"You know what? My oldest is fourteen. Not a bad looker."

Jack had seen buck-toothed Sary. He gulped and said, "She's fine, but a mite young, Fairly."

"Well, maybe. Sure blossomin' out in the chest, though. She can cook, clean, plow, make soap like her ma."

"Too young," Jack repeated. "I couldn't wait for her. I got to get settled soon."

"Well, sure, I see what you mean." Fairly debated with himself. "Tell you what. Sary'll be fifteen in December. I'll throw in that Hereford bull you wanted and some pigs and chickens."

Trapped, Jack could only temporize. "Gosh, Fairly. I'll think it over."

"Your spread's near enough to mine. Maybe we could buy out Hambone—he's shiftless. Only land between yours and mine. Put us together a real place."

Jack said, "That's real damn big of you, Fairly. I appreciate it."

"Think nothin' of it." The big man arose, beaming. "Now you got nothin' to moon about. Get yourself good and laid in Dodge. Clean out the flues. When we get home we'll talk turkey."

"Sure, Fairly. Thanks. Thanks a heap."

He turned over in his blankets and made himself lie perfectly still. Sary, he thought, my Gawd. All nobby knees and elbows and them teeth! And talk! Jabbered from early light to late dark.

He would buy his own livestock. He had water, better land than Fairly. He needed Fairly's help like woolen underwear in July.

But he did need Fairly's friendship. The older man had been good to him in a thousand ways. He couldn't insult him or hurt his feelings, or even Sary's feelings, although he would be glad to hurt the seat of Sary's pants with a good swift kick.

The situation was becoming more desperate with the days. Now, besides wanting what he wanted, he had to worry how to duck something he purely didn't want and wouldn't have. Surely, there was no more miserable trail driver in all the western land.

Kitty Devlin lay alongside Maury Dent in her neck-high cotton nightgown. She said, "I lost my knife. I showed it to you, remember? Then, when I started upstairs, I missed it. Went down and looked all around. Now, everybody knows it's my knife. Fitz told it around, to keep them from trying anything, so I wouldn't have to use it. Wouldn't you think whoever found it would give it back to me?"

Maury said, "It's probably in some corner or crack. It'll turn up."

Kitty said, "How about that Duke Parry?"

"What about him?"

"Oh, nothin'."

"Then why talk about him?" Maury couldn't sleep. She was annoyed because she shared the room with Kitty and couldn't slip down the hall without Kitty knowing about it. She moved restlessly on the bed.

Kitty said, "What's wrong with mentioning him? What's the matter with you tonight?"

"Nothing," said Maury. "Let's get to sleep. Tomorrow's another workday."

"Every day's a workday. I'm sick of it."

"The stage runs every day."

"Don't snap at me. I don't feel good, Maury. I wish . . ."

"Maybe you'd rather be in Madam Beesom's charming establishment," said Maury.

"You're being real mean. You mustn't feel so good your own self," said Kitty.

"I'll survive."

Kitty was silent a minute. Then she said, "That Duke, he dresses like a dude, but he's not a dude. Mr. Fitz thinks a heap of him, so he must be something."

"Oh, yes, I reckon he's something. A man."

"You act like men are poison or something, I do declare."

Maury said flatly, "Men are what you let them make of you."

Kitty thought this over. "Don't make sense, Maury."

"That's the point."

"Is it? Well, I don't get it."

Maury said, "Will you go to sleep?"

Not that it would do any good if Kitty did sleep, she thought. She still didn't dare chance it. First of all, she wasn't sure Duke wanted her any more. He hadn't acted as if he did. He had good reason not to want her.

If she wasn't such a coward, it might be different. She could do a lot of things if she didn't get scared at the crucial moment.

She'd have taken the laudanum if she had the nerve. She wouldn't have let Duke know she was thinking about it if she wasn't frightened. Then she would be dead and out of it all, without the memories which brought nightmares and day sweats.

She fought her nerves, lying on her side, face turned away from the girl. Kitty was already asleep, her breathing deep and healthy. Maury raised on her elbow. The starlight and a gentle moon threw enough radiance for her to see the pert, pretty face, the youthful face.

Even the texture of her skin is softer, she thought sadly. Only a few years, but it is how you spend the years. If she goes the way I did, she'll look older than I when she is my age. She's fair-skinned, the kind that go quickly.

She lay down again, remembering what the Duke had tried to teach her, trying to believe it. Everyone for himself, just so long as you obey the Golden Rule, he had said. Treat the other guy good, and when he turns on you, let him have it. Mind your own business and don't look over your shoulder, he said, and then he paid her way to Holiday.

That's what he said. She had tried and in some part succeeded. But she was still a coward and in her heart she knew it well.

Chapter 4

THE MARSHAL'S Office was a large room with a gun rack on one wall, a map of the United States on another, two windows looking out on the street, and a heavy reinforced oak door leading to the jail cells at the rear. Simon Avidon came into it on Monday morning and found Donkey behind his rolltop desk, playing with a stiletto, trying to stab flies with its point.

"What are you doing with Kitty's knife?" he demanded.

"I didn't take it offen her leg," said Donkey, smirking.

"Where did you get it?"

"Found it. She musta dropped it in the bar." He remembered a grievance and asked, "Hey! What we goin' to do about Duke?"

"Why should we do something about him?"

"Well, he whomped me down."

"You apologized for that."

Donkey puzzled this out, put the blade down on top of the desk. "That's right. I did, didn't I?"

"So forget it."

"Well, if you say so, Simon."

"You might sort of keep an eye on him, though," said Avidon. "Hang around, notice what he does. Don't breathe down his neck, now. Stay across the street, but watch him."

"Sure, I know. It gives me somethin' to do. Things been awful slow lately." Donkey took his gunbelt from a hook, dabbed at his highly polished star, and ambled out.

Avidon sat down, picking up the thin blade, feeling its needle point. His mind was still gnawing at the problem of Fitz Warren and Judge Shelley's dire prediction of failure.

If Fitz stood solidly in opposition, there would be others to follow his lead. The townspeople were apathetic in most ways because they were prosperous. They wanted nothing more than the maintenance of the status quo. They had known Fitz for many years, appreciated his kindness and his easygoing philosophy. If it came to a showdown, there was no question that they would back the owner of the Holiday House and Bar.

There must be some way that Simon Avidon could be made to shine, he pondered. He had his own few followers. If he had a peg to hang something on, he could rise to the top.

Maybe he could point this out to Fitz. If the old man realized the full import of the opportunity, how could he resist joining forces?

He could not delay, Avidon knew. The advent of Duke Parry on the scene tipped the balance, provided a possible new hero. If Fitz lined up with Parry, there would be no second place. His whole carefully constructed edifice would collapse and Simon Avidon would be buried in the ruins.

The pictures were becoming very clear.

He rose from behind the desk. He was wearing the two guns tied with thongs low on his flanks. He was the perfect symbol of the lawman. He cocked his hat and went out into the soft June sun. It was a good time to talk to Fitz, since Holiday House would be deserted at this hour.

He suddenly realized he had the poniard in his hand. He slid it into his belt, twisting it so that the sharp point did not stick against his flesh. He saw Donkey idling in front of the general store opposite the Texas Bank. The streets were still a bit damp from the early-morning dew and a slight rain which had fallen during the night. It was a pleasant, quiet Monday morning in June.

Avidon looked through the glass windows of the bank. They were clean and wide. He saw Duke Parry sitting at ease within the railing that separated Mayor Chittley's desk from the common folk. The sight annoyed him. Chittley was leaning forward, his beady eyes fixed on Parry's face, his mouth half open in the expression of cupidity which Avidon recognized.

Upon a hunch he motioned Donkey to follow him. He walked down past the millinery shop and the Chinaman's to the Holiday House and Bar. Again he gestured, and Donkey, who took orders like an obedient beast, crossed the street without haste.

Avidon said, "Stick around outside. Listen, in case I need you later for a witness. Fitz might say something we can use."

Donkey said, "I'll be there."

The Holiday House and Bar had several entrances. There was the regular front entrance to the lobby. There was a rear entrance. There was a front and a back entry to the attached barroom, which was really a separate, one-story building. It was Fitz Warren's habit to be in the bar early, making sure the swamper had cleaned up properly, for Fitz was a neat man. Avidon chose the bat-wing front entry and was about to push through when he heard Kitty's voice, too loud, strident, angry.

He stopped dead, stepped aside so that he could not be seen above or below the swinging doors from the inside. He listened.

"I know you been nicer to me than maybe I deserve. I admit it, Mr. Fitz. But I do declare, a girl's got her rights. It's not fair. Your Duke Parry, indeed!"

Fitz answered, testily for him, "All I said was that he was a good man and time he settled down, too."

"He may be everything you say. I'm not denying it. It's just that sometimes, Mr. Fitz, a girl just is not interested. A girl knows . . ."

"Like you knowed last time?"

There was a tiny silence, then Kitty's voice really went up. "That's the meanest thing you could say to me! I never thought you'd ever, ever throw it up to me! I hate you! I'm going away! I won't stay here!"

There was a sound of heels pounding as Kitty fled.

It was always good to catch a man off balance, Avidon thought. He retreated on tiptoe, then slammed his boots down hard across the wooden porch, shoving through the doors into the barroom.

Fitz was sitting at a table near the far end of the bar. His gaze was fixed on the back door, through which Kitty must have vanished on her way upstairs to weep in the sanctity of the room she shared with the dark woman. Avidon smiled his broadest and said, "Good morning, Fitz. Busy?"

The older man turned. One look at his eyes told Avidon the story, revealing the emotion behind them, opening a door through which the marshal could see quite plainly.

Fitz was in love with Kitty. There was no doubt of that. His first words dispelled any lingering question. "Were you listenin' out there, you coyote?"

"Now, just a minute, Fitz. I came in here to talk business."

The heavy man got up and came forward to within two

feet of Avidon. He was hoarse with pain and anger. "The
only business you ever got with me is over the bar. At
that, I wish you'd hang out in the Aces Up where you be-
long. I always heard, like seeks like. Whyn't you go down
there with the saddle tramps and Mexicans? You own the
place—give it a play once in awhile."

"I do not own it." He himself was suddenly on the defen-
sive, off balance. "What's got into you, Fitz? I want to make
a deal with you, a good proposition. Make us both top men
in Holiday."

"Don't babble your foolishment in my face," snarled Fitz.
"Down-at-the-heel Southerners never did suit me."

A little red light flickered, but Avidon tried to hold onto
himself. "Now, listen, Fitz. . . ."

"Aw, shut up. And get out of here. I'm sick of you and
your pulin' ways. Dam' sick!"

The unexpectedness of the attack, coming from a man
known for his forebearance and tolerance, completely unset-
tled Avidon. He said, "You better pour us a drink and start
over."

"I'm startin' over. I'm telling you. Get the hell out of here
and don't come back."

"Don't come back?" It was worse than a blow in the
face. "You mean—you're barring me from Holiday House?"

"I don't mean nothin' different."

"You—you can't do that." The world spun around and
the red spot danced in front of his eyes. If anyone ever so
much as heard of this, he was ruined. Rage flared up. "Just
because you wanted Kitty and I got her—"

He never finished. Fitz slapped him across the mouth.

His hand drove instinctively to his gun. Then he realized
with utter, final clarity that he could not gun down Fitz
Warren. He could not even strike him in return, an older
man, out of condition, a respected citizen.

Fitz turned his back in contempt, saying, "I said, 'Get
out,' and I meant it. I've been ready to run you out of town
for some time. Now's as good as any."

The hand which had strayed to the gun butt stopped at
the cartridge belt. The haft of the knife was like a hot iron
to his fingers.

He plucked it out. Now his mind was flying. The little
pieces were arranging themselves. He could read the message.

He took one quick step. He drove the knife up under the
left shoulder blade. He twisted it home, even as with the
other hand he stifled Fitz's dying outcry.

He let the heavy body drop away from him. He made sure there was no blood on him.

He ran to the door and motioned to Donkey, who was staring open-mouthed. Donkey came in, looked down at Fitz, spat calculatingly. Avidon cautioned him to silence.

He was already on his way to the back stairs. He called up softly, "Kitty!"

She must have been waiting for Fitz to call her back. She came immediately, but paused when she saw who it was.

"Mr. Fitz wants to see you," he whispered.

She came running down. He followed close behind. When she stopped at sight of Fitz's body, saw the blood, and screamed, he grabbed her.

He said, "Donkey, you heard it and saw it."

Donkey was a moment slow, then he got it in his head. "I sure did."

"I wouldn't be surprised somebody else might not have heard them arguing," said Avidon. It was working nicely, and she was too shocked to realize what was happening. "Take her down to jail. Don't let her talk to anyone until I get there."

Donkey had her in a twisted arm hold and was whisking her out of there before she screamed. Smiling sweetly, he slapped his fist against her chin, half-picked her up, and carried her out onto the street. He moved very swiftly when he wanted to, Avidon thought, or when he had a chance to hurt someone or something who couldn't fight back. He had the half-conscious girl out of sight before anyone on the nearly deserted street knew what was happening.

Avidon's pulse was beating swiftly but strongly as he moved to the door leading into the lobby. He was doing it, he thought, a pride welling within him. He was acting it out, playing the part as it unfolded. He was actually good at it.

He called, "Holy Joe! You Maury!"

Holy Joe was at breakfast. He came blinking into the lobby.

Avidon said crisply, "Get the doc. There's hell to pay. You heard Kitty yelling?"

Holy Joe swallowed egg and nodded.

"Well, she up and stabbed Fitz with that knife he gave her. In the back, at that."

Holy Joe went lumbering out of the hotel.

"Maury!" Avidon yelled. He had to know if she had been upstairs. If she had, there might be trouble about the timing. He must learn her whereabouts and act at once.

To his relief she came from the dining room. She had been

waiting on Holy Joe, he expected. He motioned to her to follow and strode confidently into the bar where Fitz Warren lay on the floor, as dead as Adam. He had it made, now. With the judge's help, he could take over. Fitz's influence was gone. He was marrying Chittley's daughter. It was better this way.

Maybe they'd hang Kitty. It wasn't beyond possibility, the way people looked up to Fitz and respected him. She'd taken his kindness and repaid him with a knife in the back. Even a woman could be hanged for that. County law was Holiday law. And there was always Royball Shelley—who didn't like women in general and Kitty Devlin in particular.

The thought excited him. To do away with Kitty forever, to put her in a grave, was to make his future all the more secure. If he could stampede the town, with the help of Donkey's testimony and the judge's legal position, it was as good as done.

Just then the doors swung open for a moment, then closed like the wings of a large bird. Avidon found himself looking squarely into the eyes of Duke Parry.

He said, "You startled me, Duke. I've got bad news for you."

Duke looked once at Fitz's body, then back at Avidon.

Avidon said hastily, "Kitty Devlin. It's her knife. I got here while they were arguing. Fitz turned his back and she let him have it."

"You saw it?"

"Donkey saw it, too." Avidon spread his hands. "Holy Joe heard them arguing. Wouldn't be surprised if the waitress did, too." He turned. Maury stood just inside the bar, her face a white blob of fear. Duke spoke.

"Stabbed him in the back." It was a quiet statement. Duke leaned over and squinted hard at the still features of his old friend. "Hard way to go, stabbed by a friend in the back."

He straightened up. To Avidon's relief he showed no high emotion, no anger.

Duke said, "Tell the doc I'll take care of funeral arrangements. Where's Kitty?"

"Donkey took her in."

Duke nodded, went toward Maury. A cold fish, thought Avidon. Seen too much sudden death. Nothing fazes him, even the stabbing of one of his oldest acquaintances.

Chapter 5

IT WAS Wednesday. Fitz Warren had been returned to the dust from which he came. Kitty Devlin had been arraigned for his murder, protesting her innocence all the while. Duke Parry sat in his room and looked out of the window at Holiday Avenue and pondered the ways of mankind.

It was gratifying, in a way, to realize how much old Fitz had meant to the town. On the other hand, it went against the Duke's grain, the way they hollered for Kitty's neck.

It was hard to believe a Texas town would have its heart set on hanging a woman. Yet peaceful, sequestered old Holiday was hellbent for a necktie party.

There was a tap on his door. He went over and unlocked it, then stepped back as Maury pushed by him, closed the door quickly, and leaned against it. Deep shadows made her face gaunt, and he remembered when he had seen her like this, in Dodge, and he knew the cause.

He said mildly, "Nobody's going to hurt you, Maury."

"You've got to believe me. Why won't you believe me?"

He sat down at the window again. She did not move from the door. He said, "Kitty could have found the knife that morning. It's the kind of thing a redhead would do. She picks it up, has it in her hand. She gets mad, strikes out."

Maury said, "Then why is it that Monk didn't find it? He swept up, mopped. Fitz was particular about the cleaning. Monk swears it wasn't in the barroom."

"Maybe she found it elsewhere."

"Duke, she didn't do it."

"Two men swear she did, that they saw it."

"You'd believe those two?"

"Not on a stack of Bibles."

"Then why don't you do something? What's got into you? In Dodge City you saved me when I wasn't worth the trouble. You went out of your way. . . ."

He said patiently, "Look down at the town. See those knots of people? They all believe she did it. If it wasn't for Judge Shelley, they'd have lynched her. Those people put a heap of store in Fitz."

"So did I. So did you. Is it doing him any good to have a woman hanged when she's innocent?"

He looked at her oddly. "Why are you so scared? Because a woman's being scragged? You think it could happen to you?"

She bit her lip. She scarcely knew why she was afraid, most of the time. "I don't know. Kitty's so young . . . and she didn't kill Fitz."

"You're real sure?" He hesitated. "You wouldn't be holding something back, would you, Maury?"

"Of course not. Why should I?"

"Reckon you're scared of Avidon and Donkey. And Judge Shelley, he'd scare any woman."

She managed to keep her face organized, but it was not easy. "I just know she didn't do it, Duke."

"The town of Holiday believes she did. It would take a strong piece of evidence to change their minds, those folks."

"You could do it."

"I have nothing to show them."

"You could stand Donkey and Avidon on their heads. You know you could."

"Not with the town behind them solid."

"They're going to hang Kitty, you know that. It makes me sick to think about it." Her mouth worked, her lips were dry.

"They never have hanged a woman in Texas."

"They did up north."

"Sure, but they caught her rustling six or seven times. Then a drunk bunch come on her with a runnin' iron, and there was a tree handy. She was an ugly old bitch, anyway."

She said dully, "You won't do anything for Kitty."

"It's your story. Tell it to the judge."

She couldn't do it. She wanted to, but Duke's attitude discouraged the small, weak urge. She watched him, churning with mixed fear and desire. Then she slipped out of the room without making a sound.

He was watching the people, half of whom he knew. They were in a dangerous mood, all right. Shelley would love to sentence the girl to death. Would Holiday allow her to be hanged?

He didn't know. Avidon and Donkey and Shelley were bad medicine. There were new people, too, strange to the old ways. It shouldn't matter to him, anyway. Fitz was dead, his tie with Holiday was gone.

He looked around, discovered Maury had left the room. She was afraid of life, afraid of death. There was nothing he could do about Maury. She was one of God's unlucky people.

He wondered why she believed that Kitty wasn't guilty. If she had some proof. . . . It sure would be a hell of a thing to hang a woman in Texas and then find out later that she was innocent.

As a matter of fact, when he thought about it, pictured it in his mind, it was a rotten thing to hang a woman, much worse than to do away with a man. He brooded over this. He had no especially high regard for women. Why, then? He wormed reason out of himself slowly, reluctantly. It had to do with motherhood. A very special thing, bearing a child, he thought gloomily. A young woman like Kitty Devlin, she would be expected to have healthy, bouncing babies.

That was as far as he got with his delving, because it occurred to him that he could not remain in Holiday and witness this thing.

It wouldn't do to have the word get out that Duke Parry had stuck around while they topped off a woman, even if she was guilty of killing Fitz Warren. If she was or was not guilty of killing his long-time friend, people might get the idea he had something to do with the hanging.

He was beginning to pack when it occurred to him that he still hadn't worried through the problem to its ultimate conclusion. He put the war bag away, sighed, and went back to the window and stood looking down. Maury had set him off. There was reasonable doubt that Kitty had murdered Fitz.

He was in it now. His honor was involved. He would have to start asking questions, nosing around, probably get himself shot at, certainly get himself cursed. He had to make an attempt at learning the truth. Either the redheaded woman had killed Fitz or she hadn't. He would, all his life, have to answer that question, to others and to Duke Parry.

It wasn't any of his business about hanging her. The thing that mattered was that this was his hometown, even if he never saw it again, which was highly possible, and that they were thinking of hanging this woman—he had to do something about it.

His hometown, and that completed the circle of his thinking. Why was Holiday precious to him? He had no family here. Fitz was dead. It was plain enough who was running things—Avidon and the judge and Chittley.

He put his gun in its pocket, adjusted his hat, and went

down into the street. Poley Meyer stopped him after a few steps and said, "What do you think, Duke? Did they really hang that woman up north? You think it's all right to hang a woman?"

"You're old enough to make up your own mind," said Duke.

He pushed past the excited old-timer and went into the general store. It was dark and cool, as it had been in his youth, but they had changed the counters and the displays, and the place contained no memories of his father and mother. It was different, brisk and cold now. It was empty in this hour of excitement, so Duke figured that it was no longer the rallying place for the town philosophers.

Mayor Roy Chittley came forward, squinted, rubbed his hands, ducked his head in greeting. "Mornin', Mr. Parry."

There was a girl in the background. One look at her and Duke knew that is where she would always be, in the shadows. Her chin was too weak, her eyes colorless, her hair drawn back too tight. Chittley made clear that this was his daughter, Faith. Then neither man paid any further attention to her.

Duke said, "What about this mess, Mayor? What's your opinion?"

"She killed him. I wouldn't interfere with the law if I could, which I can't."

"People have been talking. About Avidon and Donkey. Seems there's some don't believe them."

"Dam' fools. Why should they make up a thing like that? Everybody knows it was the woman's knife in Fitz's back."

"You think they'll hang her?"

The girl moved, then, one hand coming up to her face. Duke watched out of the corner of his eye.

The Mayor said, "Up to the judge and jury, ain't it?"

"Just wanted to get your opinion, Mayor." He bought some cartridges for the .38 and put them in his coat pocket. They sagged, spoiling the set of the jacket, which irked him. He bowed to Faith Chittley and went out into the sunshine.

Soapy Simms blocked his way. He was a heavy-set, bow-legged man with rough, red skin. "Is it true they hung that woman up north?"

Duke said, "Now what in the hell has that got to do with anything?"

"I dunno." Soapy groped for words. "Guess we shouldn't wanta be the first."

"But you don't mind being second?"

"She kilt him," said Simms. "Stobbed him in the back. You or me stobbed a man in the back, we'd hang."

"Kitty gets a trial," said Duke. "Same as you or me."

"Hell, it was her knife in his back."

Even the people who couldn't quite believe in Avidon and Donkey would not see past the circumstance of the dagger in the back, Duke thought, walking across the dusty street toward the Texas Bank. He paused a moment, looking at the marshal's office and jail building on the opposite corner of First Street and Holiday Avenue.

Then he made up his mind. He moved slowly, turning over his doubts and trying to maintain his neutrality, and came to the door which had Avidon's name painted on it. He entered, taking in every detail of the room, looking at Donkey, whose feet were on the railing as he slumped in a wide chair.

"Like to see Miss Kitty," he said without preamble.

"Can't," said Donkey. "Orders from the marshal."

Duke gave him a long, level look, then went out and retraced his steps past the bank, across Second Street, past the millinery shop, and to the office of Judge Royball Shelley.

He went in and found the jurist intent on a lawbook, at his desk. Duke said, "Well, Judge, I see you're still willing to learn."

The man's face was expressionless. "The law is written for those who read to understand . . . if they are able to understand."

"Or able to interpret," Duke corrected.

Shelley closed the book, marking his place. "As you say, Parry. What can I do for you today?"

"I want to talk to Kitty Devlin."

"Yes. You would."

"Someone ought to," Duke offered.

"You have the urge to interfere. It is part of you. It would be simpler to move on, now that Fitz is gone. You have no reason to remain here. Yet you must interpose yourself between a criminal and the law."

"Your definitions are sometimes weird," Duke said. "A murderer is not necessarily a criminal. In fact, few murderers are criminals. I would venture to suggest that careful investigation would show more criminals sitting in judgment than there are among folk charged with murder."

Shelley shook his head. "The renegade Jesuit taught you all his tricks, didn't he? You cannot bait me, Parry. I am well aware of the definition of a criminal."

"You and Father Hal never did agree. However, what I want is to see Kitty Devlin. Your marshal has left orders against it. You know and I know that he is outside his rights. Do I get to see her?"

His back still rigid, Judge Shelley leaned back in his hard chair. "If I denied you, there would be violence. You will end on some Boot Hill, you know, Parry. You are very confident in your youth and quickness of hand. But all like you go the same way."

"Not all of us. Only the drunks and the fanatics."

This time the judge winced. "Definition, again. You should have read for the law, Parry. I must say that I admire you in some ways." He scribbled on a piece of paper. "I decry you and your ilk. I hate waste. You are destructive, you are a fool. But you are direct and you are not afraid. Give this to Donkey."

"I couldn't call you a fool, Judge," said Duke. He went to the door, stopped, and looked back. Then he added very softly, "Not yet, Judge. Maybe someday."

He left the lean man staring after him with blue hatred in his eyes. He went back to the jail, showed the piece of paper to Donkey.

The deputy hesitated. Then he said, "Well. What kin we do, the judge bein' a dam' fool? You gotta leave your gun, though."

Duke took out the pistol. Donkey tossed it carelessly into a drawer.

Duke said, "If you spoil the balance of the trigger, you'll pay for a new one. Now open that damned door before I take your hogleg away from you and bend it over your head."

Donkey blinked, his mouth fell open. He found himself moving rapidly to the thick door leading to the cells, opening it. He fell back, letting Duke go on alone. He sat down, muttering to himself. It was something completely outside his comprehension that he should jump to obey a man he had just disarmed. It was confusing.

Kitty was behind thick bars which ran from ceiling to floor. Holiday had built its jail solidly, as it had everything else. The girl was paper-white; her hands shook as she came to cling to the iron struts and her lips trembled.

Duke said gruffly, for him, "They been abusin' you?"

"That Donkey." Tears came and ran down her soiled cheeks. "He hit me. He won't give me water enough to keep clean. He . . . he watches. Everything. He likes to watch."

"They haven't hired a woman to look after you?"

She shook her head, shame enveloping her.

This was the next step, Duke thought. First it was Maury. Then it was the complete, blind acceptance of her guilt by the town. Then it was Donkey, then the judge, then Donkey again. Now it was the utter desolation of the girl, the fear and shame in her. Strangely, she was attractive in her dirty, rumpled clothing, her disheveled, long red hair. She looked like a youngster abused by her elders, innocent of the cause, bewildered, lost. He felt himself being trapped.

He said, "You didn't do it." Up until then he had not been certain, but now he knew she was innocent. Maury was right, he had been stupid not to believe the frightened Maury.

"They're trying to make me say I did. The food—I can't eat it. They watch me, so that I can't sleep . . . or anything. They're trying to drive me crazy."

"Who did it?"

Even then, caged, scared, she was honest. "I don't know. Me and Mr. Fitz, we had words." She stumbled, but he knew it was not because she was lying. She finally said, "It was about you."

"Me?" This was astounding.

"He said—he thought—he loved you, Mr. Parry. And I reckon he loved me, too."

"I be damned!" Old Fitz, it was just like him. Trying to make a match, hold him to Holiday.

"I ran upstairs. Then he . . . Avidon . . . he called me. I came down, and he said I stabbed Mr. Fitz, and Donkey hit me and carried me here."

"Yeah. I guess I see it." But it wouldn't do any good. The town wouldn't believe. He asked, "What about the knife?"

"I lost it. You can ask Maury. She knew. I told her. Why hasn't Maury said anything?"

"She did. To me. That's why I'm here." No use to rehearse the other problems. He had to think more about them, anyway.

"Maury can prove I didn't have the knife. That's all that keeps me goin', Mr. Parry. Maury can prove it."

"Sure, she can." He dissembled, that she might not suspect the slender reed on which she leaned. "I'll attend to things, Kitty. You hold tight. I'll start right now."

"Don't go!" The tears came faster. "I'm . . . awful scared."

"Stop being scared," he said. "The Duke's with you."

She looked hard at him. The tears diminished. The beginning of a smile hovered on her lips. "Those are wonderful words. 'The Duke's with you.' I won't be scared, then. Thank you, thank you, Duke!"

He went to the thick door and pounded. Donkey opened it. Avidon was now sitting behind the desk. He looked cheerfully at Duke.

"So you've been visiting our canary, huh?"

Duke held out his hand. "My gun, please."

Avidon took it out of the drawer, looked at it with real curiosity. Duke leaned over and took it away from him, checked to make sure it was not unloaded, held it in his hand. Avidon's eyes grew round, and he glanced at Donkey. The deputy, his back against the door to the jail, did not stir.

Duke said, his words crackling despite himself, "You hire a woman, Avidon, to take care of Kitty."

The marshal put both hands on the desk, balancing himself, trying to hold his temper. "Now, just a minute, Duke . . ."

"You give her water. And food, for which I will pay. You treat her like any prisoner, only better."

"Now look, I'm running this office. I got reasons for what I'm doing. That bitch stabbed Fitz in the back. Fitz was a good friend of mine." He gained confidence with the knowledge that he had played it perfectly, that the town was behind him. "When she gets into court, she'll admit she did it."

"You think so?"

"I know so. I've got my own ways of handling things. Maybe they ain't exactly on the line of strict law. But you want the woman who killed your friend to get her deserts, don't you?"

The gun came up a little in his grasp, but Duke made himself put it away. He forced himself to say, "Well, lookin' at it that way, maybe you got something. O.K., Marshal."

He nodded and went out on the street.

There was no use butting his head against a stone wall. He started back to the hotel. He would have to make Maury sign a deposition. That would raise a doubt. Some few in town would then have to stop and consider the possibility of Kitty's innocence. One thing at a time, he told himself.

There was no alternative, after all. He could not gun down Avidon, Donkey, the judge, the mayor, and all of Holiday. He was absolutely sure now that Kitty did not kill Fitz. He should never have believed it. She was not the kind of girl who could do such a thing, even in rage. Maury's story was true. He would have to get to drunken old Monk, the swamper, too; not a reliable witness but some corroboration that the knife was not in the bar at cleaning-up time.

He could handle it, he thought, turning his head aside to avoid the dust kicked up by the stage going north. It was all a matter of bucking up Maury until she had the nerve to tell her story openly, to sign her name to it.

For the hundredth time he wondered what had long ago

put the fear into Maury and started her on the run. It was a terrible thing to happen, because there were so many sterling qualities in the woman. If she could ever get herself together, she would be something, as he well knew. He had never known a better companion, in or out of bed, when the black mood was not on her.

He went up the stairs of the hotel on the run. He went past Holy Jim, who was tending the desk, into the dining room. Monk, bleary-eyed, shuffling, was mopping the floor.

"Where's Maury?"

"Gone," said Monk. "Purely gone. She sure had nice ankles, didn't she, Duke. Gal had the purtiest ankles I ever did see."

"Gone? Gone where?"

Monk made a swirl with the mop. "Who knows where a woman goes? Such ankles! Seen her leg once, when she was goin' upstairs. Some gal, Maury!"

Duke went out to the desk. "Where did Maury go?"

Holy Jim took a note from the drawer. "Left this for you, Duke. Guess she didn't like Kitty bein' jailed. She looked pretty bad."

"Where did she go?"

"Why, she took the stage that just left. Northbound through the Territory. Reckon she's headin' for Dodge."

He felt drained, standing there. He nodded, went up the stairs slowly to Room Nine. He sat down on the bed. It was hopeless without Maury. He knocked from his hat some of the dust stirred up by the stage she had taken. Monk's story was no good without Maury's corroboration. Kitty was as good as hanged right now.

The note was brief: "They'd hang me, too. It's a vigilante case, Duke. I don't dare. I don't dare do anything, do I?"

He wondered if she had taken the blue laudanum bottle back to Dodge with her.

Chapter 6

AFTER DARK, Duke thought, evil deeds seem reasonable. The calm, solid town of Holiday had suffered a sad change. He walked the streets in shadows, listening, hearing nothing to lighten the burden which pressed more heavily on him with each hour.

He moved across from the jail, studying the building. It was invulnerable, that was obvious. He crossed the street to the edge of town and slid into the Aces Up Saloon.

The place was crowded with cowboys, farmhands and, at one end, a bit apart from the other customers, there was a group of Mexicans. He made his way unnoticed to a place behind these dark-skinned, silent people and ordered a bottle of beer, mistrusting the whisky. No one noticed him.

He heard Donkey's voice, drunken, slurring his words, loud. "They stretched that woman in Washin'ton, didn't they? The one was in the Abe Lincoln business? Mrs. Suratt."

"Shoulda give her a medal," said a bewhiskered Texan whom Donkey called "Sledge." He had an idiot's leer.

A Yankee with a high, nasal twang said, "Dam'f they shoulda."

Donkey interposed quickly, "They stretched her neck. If the Gov'ment can do it, what's wrong with it?"

"Not a buggered thing," said Yankee, joining Donkey with celerity. "No difference. Man or woman."

Sledge giggled over his red whisky. "Well, some difference. I figure to be in the front row."

"Wanta see her kick?"

"She'll be wearin' drawers, Sledge."

"Tie their skirts down. To the ankles," said another citizen. "No peep show, Sledge."

"Jedge wouldn't stand for it."

48

"Not the jedge. He's all legal."

Sledge's voice went up, "Mebbe the jedge won't have no say."

Donkey leaned over and slapped hard at the whiskery face. "None o' that. Me and the marshal, we're holdin' her. Nobody in this goddam town is gonna take her away."

"Want her all for yourselves?" hooted a voice from the rear.

"Yeah, Donkey, what about that?"

"You and the marshal gettin' yours?"

"Gal can't say no. Not where she is."

Donkey smirked. "Now, you know that ain't legal. This here whole rangdoodle is gonna be legal. Judge says so. Marshal says so."

A Mexican stirred. His eyes were brown and slanted, his mouth beneath a flowing mustache curled in a sneer. As he turned away, Duke followed him. They went out a side door into an alley.

The man said, "Señor Duke."

"That's me. Do I know you?"

"Arimendez. Many years, now, señor."

"Arimendez. Your father had a farm?"

"The same."

They shook hands. "You still on the old place?"

"Where else?"

"Just outside town, if I remember."

"They buy my vegetables. It has always been a good place."

A group of men went by the mouth of the alley. One said, "I say when a woman stops bein' a woman, she ain't no different from a man."

"Oh, they'll hang her, all right," said another.

Duke looked at his companion. "Not such a good place now, though."

"The marshal, he is a bad man, señor. About this stabbing, I do not know. But the marshal has no good in him."

"Check," said Duke. He hadn't played chess since Father Hal's death. His mind was beginning to work clearly again. Maury's departure had left him few alternatives. But he was planning.

"If it were to hang the woman, then the law is enough. The talk, that is bad, eh?"

"Your father was a gentleman, too," said Duke.

"Gracias, Señor Duke. He was not allowed to drink in Holiday House, either."

"Texas," nodded Duke. "Nobody can do anything about Texas."

"I have thought of going away. But this is our land. My woman, my children, they know nothing of what I feel. Maybe things will change."

Duke asked suddenly, "You got a horse, amigo?"

"Three horses. One good enough to ride."

"No good," Duke said. "Now that I think of it. They'd know it was gone."

"Si, señor, no good."

Duke felt the roll of bills in his pocket. "I could steal him. But maybe they wouldn't believe it."

"They would not believe."

"Yea. Well, I'll have to move around some more."

Arimendez held him by the sleeve. "I will give you the horse."

"No. It would make another wrong. You have a family. It would be a bad swap."

Still the man held him. "Señor."

"Yes?"

Arimendez chuckled. "I have thought. Judge Shelley has a fine horse."

Duke laughed aloud, the first time since Fitz's death. "You don't say? Where does he keep it?"

"The livery stable. In a special stall. Not with other ponies. Special—in the back."

"I'll take a look." He shook the man's hand again. "Thanks a heap, Arimendez. If you ever want to get out of here, write me care of the Long Branch in Dodge City."

The wide sombrero wagged negation. "It has been a nice town. I am known here. They do not harm me. Someday, maybe, my children will walk on the boards, their heads high."

Arimendez melted into the darkness, going behind the saloon building, across lots toward his little piece of land. Possibly, thought Duke, he was the one man in town who could have helped at this moment. If his resolution needed hardening, the quiet words of the Mexican contrasted to the bombast of the barroom crowd had accomplished it.

He went toward the livery stable at the far end of the street. It was inconvenient, to say the least, he thought. There was the matter of a saddle.

People were milling up and down; no one in Holiday seemed to be minding his own business tonight. He knew there must be some in town who did not fall in with the rank and file. There was probably a considerable body of them, staying at home, keeping out of it. There might even be a few who were outraged. Certainly Judge Shelley had never been the ideal man to many.

The trouble was that he had been away too long and he did not have time to politick around and learn who was on what side. He came to Second Street and paused in front of the barbershop. There was a light in the back room, and he remembered that a poker game always was going, with Shattuck, the barber continually losing his profits. He debated, then decided not to go in. Shattuck and his cronies were aging gossips, devoid of muscle.

At Third Street there was the Wells Fargo office; it was from here that Maury had departed on the stage. He cursed her in his mind. The bakery was on the corner of Fourth, across from Holiday House. Next door was the smithy, and the livery stable was next to the only empty lot on Holiday Avenue, alongside the hotel.

He went across the street. A Negro boy named Lump was in charge. Duke gave him a dollar and looked at his own horse, which was well-groomed, well-fed, restive.

The stable had wide doors at either end. Duke went out the rear and there was a shed. Lump, following him, said, "Jedge Shelley's hoss, suh. Mighty special-like."

"Good horse?"

"Fancy."

"Gelding?"

"Whazzat? Oh . . . yassuh. How you know that?"

"I know Judge Shelley pretty good."

The boy guffawed. "Reckon you do, Mr. Duke."

"How late you keep open?"

"Well, it's accordin'. I sleeps mighty good. If I sleeps a lot daytime, I don't close up 'til I sleepy again."

Duke said, "I see. Guess you'll be up late tonight."

"Naw. I didn't sleep so good today. People moseyin' around, talkin' about hangin' and such, kept me awake."

"O.K., Lump." He fished out another dollar. "That the Judge's saddle, on the wooden horse?"

"Yassuh. Jedge mighty partic'lar about that saddle. All silvered up. He don't ride much, but he purty when he ride."

Duke gave him the dollar. "Sleep tight, Lump."

"I always does. Thank you, Mr. Duke."

He went across the empty lot, in the back way and up to his room. He had taken the key with him when he left. He poured water into the basin, stripped down, and got out his soap and began washing himself all over. He could think better when he was clean, he always believed.

Simon Avidon went into the jail block and looked at the tray from the Chinaman's. Kitty had eaten it all, the best the restaurant had to offer. She had managed to fix her hair up on top of her head and was clean again, too. When he opened the door of her cell, she shrank far back to the corner and faced him.

He said, "Well, now, Kitty. Just you and me."

"Don't forget Duke Parry," she managed to say.

"Oh, sure, the Duke. He sent you the food and all. Asked us to get a woman in here, too. You notice I sent Donkey away."

"You dirty, scheming rat," she said.

"Is that the way to talk to an old . . . friend?" he asked softly. "Honest, Kitty, after what we've been to each other, I should think you'd know me better."

He walked close to her and slapped her face, hard, with his open palm. She slumped against the wall, dazed.

He went on, "You shouldn't talk like that after I fed you good, let you wash up and all."

"You murderer," she said. It didn't make any difference when she died, she thought. If he killed her now, people would know, they'd get after him. "You slimy, foul snake."

"Now, now. You killed Fitz, remember?"

"You killed him. The only way you know how . . . from behind."

This amused him. He smiled and said, "Donkey saw you do it. You want me to send for Donkey, let him loose with you? Alone, with no one to know? Donkey has peculiar ways of enjoying himself."

"You don't dare!"

"Oh, yes, I do. You got to get it in your head, Kitty, that I'm running this place. I'm the boss."

"You're filth!"

He slapped her again, but without much violence. "Manners, Kitty, manners. Now you know you killed Fitz. Why don't you admit it?"

"Scum." She was mumbling through aching lips.

"It would make everything so much nicer if you just signed a paper. I've got it all written out for you." He took it from his pocket and unfolded it. "Just sign at the bottom."

She tried to grab it from him, but he held it out of reach.

"I didn't think you were quite ready. After tomorrow, you will be."

"I'll see you fry in hell first!"

"I've got to explain things." He sat down on the bunk and spoke slowly and clearly. "You see, if you go into court and deny you killed Fitz, there'll be a trial. You haven't got a chance, Kitty. The jury will convict you. Then Judge Shelley will sentence you to hang by the neck until you are dead, dead, dead."

She was hypnotized by the menace in the last words. Once she had heard the judge condemn a rustler in exactly that tone. Could it really happen to her? Would she really be led out before all the people, a rope around her neck?

He said, "On the other hand, if you confess, all neat and legal, it'll be different. There won't be a trial, or fuss with people, and the judge'll merely send you to jail for life."

She knew better than that. She had sense enough not to shout it at him, but she was aware that while she was alive Avidon was in danger. There was always the chance that someone, somewhere might believe her. If she went on the stand and accused him, she might be disbelieved, even hanged, but the shadow of the doubt would lay over Avidon forever.

She said merely, "I'll never sign it."

"Too bad," he sighed. "Tomorrow, when Donkey's feelin' randy, it'll be hard on you."

"You don't dare," she said again, knowing he did dare.

"He hurts people. Funny thing about old Donkey, he can't have any fun unless somebody's being hurt."

"Duke Parry will kill you."

"I take it that Duke is my successor," said Avidon. "That's just right for him, my leavings. I'm not worried about him, you know. Too many people are on my side. Duke won't try anything. He's too smart."

"You'll see." She tried to conceal her growing panic.

"Besides, who'll believe you? Or him? You're in the hands of the law, Kitty. Can't you get that into your dumb head?"

She said, "I know your law."

"You think you know all about me, don't you?"

"All that I need to know." She couldn't say more. A black cloud was settling over her. Apathy was taking over.

He saw this, with his usual power of discernment. Threats wouldn't work now, he knew. Tomorrow he would have to go through with it, put Donkey in there with her.

He arose, went out, and locked the cell behind him. He jingled the keys. "The sign of authority. While I have these, you haven't got a chance. Better think hard tonight: jail, or a rope around that pretty neck. I'll check with you early in the morning, real early. Before people are up. Donkey'll have a better chance, that way. Sleep tight, Kitty."

She sank back, staggered to the bunk, hunched on its edge.

There had been no further word from Duke. He had sent the food, and water to wash with. But he hadn't been to see her again. He was smart, and hard, like Avidon said. Maybe it was too much for him. Maybe he couldn't handle it, a whole town and the law of the town.

And Maury, she thought. Where was Maury? Why hadn't she come forward? The Duke could protect her. There were good people who would at least listen to Maury and the Duke and old Monk. Every case had two sides.

It was no use. The sound of jangling keys rang in her head. Avidon was in charge.

It was impossible, but it was true. The first man with whom she had ever had relations was going to hang her. The man she had loved—and she had loved him—was contriving the most ignoble of deaths for her.

She writhed; she had an impulse to tear off her clothes, so stained and soiled, to scream and beat on the walls of the cell. She started up, rigid, her hands clawing.

Then she found something inside her. She seemed to break through a veil. She was scared to her shoes, but there was a release. She lay down on the bunk. She relaxed her taut muscles.

If she had to die, even at the end of a rope, then she would do it her way. If she had to endure Donkey, she would find some way to manage it. She would fight as long as possible. They would have to kill her against her will and strength.

She would never quit. Her father may have been a stolid Main lobersterman and fisherman, but he was strong. He was tough. Her mother had been a farm girl. There was blood in her which had defied the elements themselves for generations.

She smiled weakly, and her eyes closed. She slept.

Chapter 7

THURSDAY WAS a workday, so the town was quiet long before midnight except for the motley crowd of drinkers and idlers and part-time handy men in the Aces Up Saloon. Duke packed his possessions into the saddlebags, saw to his rifle and revolver. He was wearing dark-colored range clothing.

He had no definite plan. He saw no way to accomplish that which he must do. If he was to be the instrument of Fate, in which Father Hal had believed, he was a blunt one, he thought.

He went down the back stairs carrying his gear. He made his way across lots, unobserved, to the stable. He saddled his horse and hitched him opposite the special lean-to which sheltered the gelding belonging to Judge Shelley. He thrust his rifle into the boot and returned to Holiday Avenue. There was no human in view, only a dog sniffing the gutters.

He walked past the hotel and the Chinaman's, paused in front of the judge's office. There was no light from the living quarters of Royball Shelley.

A hooded figure came out of Second Street, and Duke waited, stepping into the shadows. In a moment he saw that it was Faith Chittley. He waited for her to go across the street in the direction of the store.

She moved with quick little steps, like a hurrying child. She whispered, "I saw you coming down the avenue."

"Yes, ma'am?" Even her voice was disembodied, without weight or resonance.

"Papa says they will surely hang her."

"I believe him." He had to think, to get away from this weak young girl.

55

"Simon says they won't, but he doesn't mean what he says." The voice gained strength. "Simon is a liar, Mr. Parry."

"Yes. Simon is a dangerous man."

"They'll make me marry him." She paused. "You don't know my mother. Sometimes *I* don't know her. My mother is sick, She thinks Simon will be rich, and she wants me to be with the rich, strong people."

She had caught his interest with her first reference to Avidon. He said, "Does your mother know you're here?"

"They think I'm in bed. I tried to see the judge. I talked to people. They're going to hang her. I just left Simon."

Duke said, "He lied to you."

"Yes." From under the shawl which hooded her thin shoulders she reached out a hand. Unbelieving, he took from her a set of keys. "He has two sets. Simon is very careful. Once he lost the keys, and it was a bit embarrassing—some people even laughed at him."

Duke said, "What were you going to do with them?"

"Find you."

"But how could you know I'd do anything?"

"Someone has to," she said simply.

He took a deep breath. "I been fooled plenty times, Miss Chittley. This beats everything."

"It's not only the woman," she said carefully. "Although that is bad enough. You see, I don't want to marry Simon. I don't want to marry anyone I have met so far."

"Yes. I see." His mind was racing. "Look, Kitty's clothes are in bad shape. Can you help me there?"

"Oh! I hadn't thought of that." The cowled head shook back and forth. "That's just like me. Never thinking. I could —do you think she could wear mine?"

"Anything will have to make do."

"Where should I bring them?"

"You know where the judge keeps his horse?"

"Everyone knows that."

"Make a tight bundle. Tie it tight. Meet me there."

"I can do that." She shook her head again. "Tonight I can do anything." She peered at him in the shadows. "Mr. Parry, did she kill Mr. Fitz?"

"No."

"Then—Simon or Donkey killed him."

"You've got a quick mind."

"No one else was there. It's really very simple. I'm afraid I'm a simple person."

"Not tonight, Miss Chittley."

She considered this. He imagined she smiled in the darkness; she stirred a bit beneath the shawl. "No. Maybe not tonight."

She seemed to flit across the street, not touching the dust with the hem of her long skirt. He looked down at the keys in his hand.

Arimendez came from the alley next to the Texas Bank. He called softly in Spanish, and Duke answered him. They walked without words to First Street, across from the jail.

It was a solid building. Both Avidon and Donkey were inside, armed with a dozen weapons.

Arimendez said, "I could not sleep, you see."

"Your family sleeps. You had better join them."

"No, señor."

Duke said, "Look, amigo, I've got the keys. I'm going in. That's all right—either it'll work or it won't. If you go in, that's different."

"Si, señor. Because of the family. However, there is the matter of the horses."

"I'll get them when I need them."

"But I sold the judge the gelding," said Arimendez. "It is an animal well known to me. Also, señor, I saw the girl and listened to what you said. There is the matter of the clothing." He produced a small package. "Bread, and cheese from the goats. You remember how the people once complained about the goats? I keep them in the hills, now."

There it was. The colorless girl and the gentlemanly Mexican offered him help. He glanced involuntarily toward heaven. The blunt instrument had been given a sharpened point.

Duke said, "Go with God, amigo. We meet at the stable."

He watched Arimendez melt into the darkness of back ways. He remembered hunting with him, the young son of a mustachioed dirt farmer, years ago, and the way the dark lad had proved his part-Indian ancestry on the trail of cougar. Duke might have to return to Holiday someday, after all. He seemed to be piling up debts.

He glanced up at the stars. There was a quarter moon, but it was partially obscured by puffy little clouds. It might rain. He had to think of a line of retreat. There was little choice. The roads were not safe. It had to be cross country. He thought of the old Chisholm Trail, but there were disadvantages because of the woman.

No, he thought, it would have to be the Western Trail. They would have a chance if they could obscure their tracks for a certain period of time, or if they could ride hard enough and fast enough to get into Indian Territory. Then on to Dodge, where he could worry it out with the advice of Bat and maybe the Earps, if they were still around.

It was in no way certain. The forces of law and order were against the girl. Warrants, extradition, all could be managed by the judge.

There was Maury, of course, but she was scared, and distance from Holiday guaranteed nothing so far as she was concerned. She might even go on, to Denver, to the Northern towns.

He examined the keys and decided which one would gain him admittance to the outer office, which one to the cells. There could be no doubt, he thought. The smaller one would get him inside the building.

He slid like a thief to the door. He used the supple strength of his gambler's hand to insert the key. He sweated a little for fear the hinge would creak. He exerted controlled deftness, twisting it, turning the knob, easing open the door inch by inch.

He was immediately aware of a night oil lamp, turned very low. It gave him the light he needed. He closed the door behind him with as much care as he had opened it. He looked at Donkey, asleep on a makeshift cot. There was no sign of Avidon, but a sound from within the cells reassured him. No woman snored with such vehemence.

He debated briefly, then decided not to take chances with Donkey. He stood over the deputy, chose his spot. He hit the man behind the left ear with the muzzle of his revolver. Donkey made no sound.

The door to the cells was a problem. It was huge and heavy, and the key stuck. He called on all his dexterity, his heavy shoulder muscles bulged. In the end it was no use. There was no chance of a silent entry.

He leaned against the unlocked portal. He shoved with his left shoulder, springing past the swinging, whining weight, landing within, feet spread, revolver poised.

Avidon was in the end cell, one removed from Kitty. He came up, gun in hand, staring, from deep sleep.

Duke said, "Drop it or take it."

Avidon dropped the gun with a clatter on the floor. The hammer slammed on the empty chamber. Duke sighed with relief.

Avidon started to rise from the cot, changed his mind. He stammered, "What . . . you can't. . . . You're crazy. . . ."

"I'm here. I can. I won't say I ain't loco," said Duke. He

was beginning to feel cheerful, high, as though he had taken several drinks.

Kitty called, "Duke, is it you? You've come for me?"

"Steady." He detected hysteria in her voice. He moved crabwise to her cell, unlocked it. Avidon was wakening, his mind was working again. Duke said, "Come out. Stay behind me."

He walked her back to Avidon's chosen bedchamber. The marshal was careful not to make a move, holding his hands half-raised.

Duke said, "Into the office."

Avidon came out, went ahead. Duke rummaged in the desk, found handcuffs. He snapped them on Avidon's wrists, located a reata, tied the marshal to his chair. He found leg irons and another pair of manacles. Donkey groaned while he was being secured.

Avidon said nothing. Donkey awakened and started to yell as Duke shoved a rag into his mouth, gagged him.

"Your deputy hasn't got as much sense as you," Duke observed. "Reckon he don't think I mean business."

"If I yelled, you'd kill me," said Avidon. "If I keep quiet, I'll see you hanged along with Kitty."

"Like I said. You got brains." Duke moved to the rifle rack. He broke the locks on all the guns with sharp, skillful blows of a Colt's .45 which he had taken from a gun belt hanging from a peg. "On the other hand, you got to catch a thief before you can hang him."

Avidon's grin might have been disconcerting under other circumstances. Still, it meant something, Duke knew. The man could think hard, straight, and fast.

Kitty said, "Can't we go?"

"Just want to make sure of some things." Duke found several boxes of .44 shells which would fit his Remington rifle. He pocketed them. "One of these, should you catch up, might have your name on it," he told Avidon. "I'm like you, some ways. I'm a careful man."

"Not careful enough," said Avidon easily.

"Could be." He found a kerchief and a wad of oily cloth used for cleaning guns. "Sorry about the way this'll taste. While you're chewin' on it, think about something, just for me."

Avidon stared at him, his lip curled. "I'll be thinkin' about the day I catch up with you."

"O.K. Just go one step further: Remember that I know you killed Fitz. Right now you've got this town buffaloed. You got law, you got everything. I'll be on the run. Then there'll be another day." He paused a moment, his voice deepened, his throat swelled. "I'll be back, Avidon. Think good about that. I'll be back."

He rammed the rag into the man's mouth. He thought that Avidon might have yelled then, from some desperate inner impulse, but he choked the thick neck, roughly fastening the gag into place. It would have been easy to kill, in that moment. It was an effort to refrain, to keep things in proper sequence.

He turned to the girl. She was shivering, but he thought she could make it. He said, "Well, now, we'd better mosey along."

She responded to his easy tone. They went out the door and onto Holiday Avenue without another look behind them. He whisked her down First Street and behind the bank. He supported her across the back lots, around behind Holiday House and Bar. She hesitated there, but he said, "Can't risk gettin' your things. Got to move."

At the stable, there was Arimendez. He held two packages. He said, "I sent the girl away."

"Maury?" said Kitty quickly. "Maury can clear me."

"Maury is gone," said Duke briefly. "We've got to ride."

The silver saddle of the judge shone on the dark gelding. Kitty recoiled.

Duke said, "We got clothes for you, food, everything. Climb on and let's make tracks."

Kitty turned a face white in the starlight. "I can't ride a horse!"

Both men stared.

"I came out here from Maine. We've got no horses in Maine. Boats—I know about boats. Nobody ever taught me to ride." She was weeping. "Can I help it? I can't help it. I'm—I'm scared of horses."

Arimendez was already in action. "The gelding was broken to harness," he said as he ran to a two-seater buckboard backed against the wall.

"My nag, too, almost," said Duke. Gloom settled on him. Fate had been too kind, too soon. A person who couldn't ride was beyond his comprehension. No wonder Avidon had given him the laugh. Trying to ride out of the pursuit of a posse with a woman was bad enough—with a woman who feared horses it was impossible.

With a buckboard it was also impossible.

Arimendez was already reaching down harness. Lump, the hostler, came rubbing his eyes, recognized Duke.

"You hirin' a rig, Mr. Parry?"

Duke started to give him money, hesitated. Would they believe that Lump was simple enough to hire out a rig at night with the judge's horse attached? There were other animals in the stable, not so fast, not so durable, hacks to pull a buckboard.

Duke said sorrowfully, "Lump, this is a shame. Here." He gave the colored boy money. "Hide this. Tell no one where you got it."

Then he hit Lump on the head. He caught the body, bore it tenderly back to the stable, deposited it in a stall. It took only a few moments to find rope and tie arms and legs. He hated to gag the unconscious hostler, but knew he must. There were unhappy angles to a jail break, he thought.

When he returned to the rear yard, the horses were hooked to the rig. They were unhappy, restive, resentful of the harness, but they stood well enough. Arimendez had his saddle and the other gear stowed in the back seat. Kitty was perched, hanging on already with both hands.

Duke paused, thrust money upon Arimendez. "In case of trouble. Otherwise, you can return it."

"No, señor."

"It is necessary, for my honor," said Duke, words he could not have spoken in English, but which sounded well in the Latin tongue. "I promise you, I will be back."

Arimendez reluctantly stowed away the bills. "For your honor, señor."

They shook hands, then Arimendez said softly, "The trail, I think, Señor Duke. First a feint, then the new trail."

"Yes. I imagine Avidon will figure it out, too, is the only trouble."

"There is no other way."

He gathered up the lines. He turned the horses in the yard. They were skitterish, strange to one another, yet he managed them without jamming the pole into a corner of the barn, for the moment a likely accident. Arimendez was already out of sight when he turned into Holiday Avenue and headed north.

Kitty sat tightly, her feet braced. He said to her, "You'll wear yourself out in a mile that way. We got a spring action on this rig. You got to give to it." He chuckled and added wryly, "Like ridin' a horse, sorta."

She gave a small gasp, then tried to relax. He drove slowly, with care, letting the horses suit their gaits to one another. There were no lights, and nothing stirred except the dog, who left his gutter to snap at the wheels of the buckboard.

They were out of town as suddenly as though they had gone

over a cliff. There were only the stars and the moon, now a sliver of white, and the road to the north over which Maury's stage had traveled. For a moment he thought of trying to catch the stage, realized it was impossible. Alone he might have made it. With the woman and the buckboard he had no chance against the stage relays.

He plotted the course of the stageline in his head. He searched vainly for the rain clouds. He couldn't remain long on the road. He would have to use his knowledge of country-side, rusty after ten years, to make the run.

It was an unlikely, clumsy way to go, he thought, wishing the girl would stop bumping and adjust herself to the spring of the wagon. He clucked to the horses, and they picked up speed. Holiday fell swiftly behind.

Chapter 8

A T DAWN the herd was already moving. Fairly was concerned with the distance to the next water hole, near the border of Indian Territory. Jack Budington rode drag for awhile to see that everything was caught up. The chuck wagon bounced past him on the left, and he covered his mouth with the kerchief and spurred his pony.

Fairly was pulled up, squinting, half-satisfied. "Got it figured to the hour. Nothin' downs me more'n to drive ganted cattle. If we was winterin', it would be different. Every pound we lose offen 'em is money when we're shippin'."

"Sure," said Jack. "We'll stretch it nice and easy."

"Drivin' herd is what you make it," said Fairly solemnly. "You got to do the job right. Reckon it's a religion to me."

"Everybody knows you're the top trail boss."

Fairly looked pleased, too pleased. "You been thinkin' some of Sary?"

"Huh? Oh—sure, I been thinkin' some." He would have to maintain some distance between himself and Fairly, he realized. The closer he got to the man, the more dangerous it could be. There was room for few ideas in Fairly's skull. The cattle drive, his family, and his ranch took up every bit of room in that round, hard skull.

"Well, you keep thinkin'. Because I got a big hunch that's the way it's goin' to be. That's the way the big outfits form up. Two smart fellers decide to throw in together, they get it made. You and me, Jack. I'm the oldest, of course, I'd run things. No more'n right."

"Sure," said Jack absently. Fairly was getting to be purely gabby. A man stored things up. Years of riding range alone,

63

sleeping out at night, working more with beast than man, it got a man thinking and thinking.

Take Jack himself—he hadn't thought about wiving before this trip. Not solid thinking, anyway. Just sort of something to do, someday, when the time was right. Women never had bothered him too much, outside the regular way a man went about it, like anybody else.

Fairly said, "Sary'll do all right. She's got the gumption. We'll have the land and the cattle. Yup, more I think on it, the better I see it."

"Well," said Jack. He shut his mouth tight. He looked afar, seeking escape. He saw Bull, the big, meaty dunderhead, ignoring a steer which might well lead a small sag off to the east. "Got to check that Bull into line. Talk to you later, Fairly."

He rode away. It was a caution, the way a man could move in on you, a man you'd known and got along with for years. Trouble was, he liked Fairly, he was more or less indebted to him for small favors. Two hundred head was no great shakes to drive to market, and Fairly was good enough to make it sound big, like Jack was somebody, or at least was going to be somebody. Come to think of it, Fairly was the one suggested he join this drive with his little herd.

But Sary—he'd rather sell the ranch and go back to workin' for forty and found. He'd rather run away to Wyoming or any dang place. He'd rather be dead than listen to a yappin' female of any age, size, or description for the rest of his life. Women weren't made for talk, in spite of their own ideas on the subject.

He visualized his perfect woman, a silent, dark, adoring creature with large bosoms and white skin, a soft woman, all smiles and sweetness—and mainly silent. Except when he wanted to chat a little, when she would agree with him, of course. Or when she suggested they go to bed early or like that. . . .

Bull was off and after the steer and a few straggling followers by now, and Jack swung wide to head them. He fired a couple of shots, hoorahed, swung his hat, and otherwise made a great show of riding hard. This was to impress Fairly. He couldn't have the foreman believing he had run out on him.

He made so much noise that Al came in from the point, a lean, laconic veteran, and the few stragglers were turned back without trouble.

Jack said, "Didn't mean to start a ruckus. Fairley's plumb set on not runnin' weight off 'em."

Al grunted, then said, "Fairly's right," and rode away.

They were in rolling country, red clay, scant water in this season but not desert. With irrigation, Jack thought, this could be ranch land. Soon they would be in the Territory for a few miles, then in Kansas. They were in good shape, all told.

Bull and Al rode back to their positions. Jack remained on the eastern flank. His mind was wandering again. He was beginning to worry about himself and these day and night dreams of women.

When he saw the red-haired girl and the man carrying a rifle walk over a knoll and stand against the skyline, the wind whipping her skirts against her nubile body, he thought it was part of the dreaming and almost rode on.

Simon Avidon did not panic for some time after Duke had left. Then the taste of the oil made him ill, and he almost choked to death on his vomit. This caused him to writhe with such violence that the chair fell over. He escaped a broken bone by some miracle and lay still, fighting for control. He could see Donkey struggling with his bonds on the cot, the metal clanking, Donkey making strangled noises against the gag.

It was best to lie still, to keep thinking, planning. His knowledge that Kitty could not ride a horse, his belief that Duke had played right into his hands, should sustain him. He tried to ease his position, knowing there were hours to endure before someone came and found the door locked and no answer and had sense enough to do something about it.

He accumulated the good things and dwelt on them: A posse would be a cinch to raise, the only problem would be selection. He would keep it small and select.

The pursuit should be easy enough. There was only one way the Duke could go—out of Texas fast, which meant the Territory. Handicapped by Kitty, Duke could not travel fast enough to get much of a lead. There were trackers who could not be fooled; there must be an expert in the posse. One day should be enough.

The ending was predictable. There would be men who grew angry at the chase, in whom the blood lust would hit boiling point if they were properly exercised. Simon Avidon had ridden with posses before. The sense of outrage at fleeting fugitives was common to them all. Their hatred mounted with each hour the pursuit was prolonged. The use of a rope and a tree limb seemed justified by their effort.

There was also tradition behind the act of lynching by
a posse. As individuals, none of the posse would think of
killing a man and a woman outside due process of law.
As a posse—a mob with badges—it became proper to kill.

Funny thing, he thought, he had never known a posse
member to regret a lynching in which he had taken part.
In fact, he had heard many a long, dull bragging tale of how
a rustler—suspected or proven—had been strung up by
otherwise eminently respectable members of Western com-
munities. It was like lynching a Negro in the South, it
fulfilled the inner needs of the sort of man who ran with the
pack.

It might be a bit different with Kitty. On the other hand,
it might be easier, if properly handled. Donkey could be
depended upon there.

If lynching a woman did prove too much for their bellies,
there could be an accident. He could call upon Donkey. He
looked across the room and saw that this was true—that is,
if Donkey didn't kill himself trying to get loose of those
irons.

He returned to the plan of action he would follow after
being released. He needed sleep and wished he could manage
an hour or so. He again had to fight the fear and discom-
fort and odd feeling of desolate helplessness. Over and over
he estimated the time it would take Kitty and Duke to make
so many miles, how much faster the posse could travel, where
they would, inevitably, come together. He forced himself
to work out each detail, to recite the names of the men he
wanted along, the matter of guns to replace those Duke had
wrecked; he even speculated on whether there would be at
the golgotha a tree with a hanging limb.

Royball Shelley awoke earlier than usual. He made a wood
fire in the little round stove and put water on for his shave
and coffee, which he made each morning in defense against
the chicory served by the Chinaman. He dressed with care,
went out onto Holiday Avenue for a look at the sky, returned to sit at his desk.

There were many pleasing things in his mind. His health
was good, the doctors thought his lung had healed. His
pocketbook was as fat as need be. Simon was running true
to form, really able in his field of local politics.

And the woman was in jail.

He had the fate of the woman well in control. With Simon's aid, he could manage it.

He heard the water boiling and went back and brewed the

coffee. He walked about lightly, feeling young. He almost wished he was back home, then laughed, realizing that Alabama was the past, that it was no longer a place important to him. He had been in Holiday for fifteen years, since he was twenty-five, and he had avoided trouble and made himself a position here.

He drank the coffee, which invigorated him even further. He decided to take a walk. Maybe it would be wise to visit Simon. He could take a secret look at the woman in her cell.

He put on his hat and went down the street. Simon did not answer the knock at the door. He was about to turn away, having no stomach for Donkey at this hour, when he heard thumping sounds. In an instant he foresaw trouble.

Prudently, he walked the length of the avenue to the smithy across from the livery stable. They returned together, Hampton, the wide, squat man of muscle, and the tall, lean judge. They entered the marshal's office.

Avidon's first words were, "Get the town up. Get horses, guns. I'll be ready in an hour."

No need to look in the cells, thought the judge. Time to act. He felt faint at the thought, the long ride, the dust and confusion, the hurly-burly of action. He left Avidon talking to Donkey and Hampton and went to the livery stable.

Thus he found Lump, bruised and incoherent. He went out back and looked at the empty stall. His gelding was gone.

He almost wept.

The horse had meant a lot to him. It had made him feel adequate. He had experienced a lot of trouble learning to ride; truthfully, he was afraid. The accomplishment had restored faith in himself at a time when he badly needed it. The gelding was the first horse he had ever owned.

When he had learned what he could from Lump, he added Duke Parry to his list of inner hates. It was not a very long list. He could not afford to hate, he was a man of terrible passions which drained him. But Duke would pay, sooner or later, for making him feel this way.

When he got back to his office, the posse was already forming. Avidon had provided Donkey with a list. Poley Meyer was out, and Soapy Simms. Sledge, drunk from the night before, was waving a revolver, uttering threats. Yankee rode up on a rabbity roan pony. And there were others of that ilk. Simon was choosing well.

No substantial citizen was in the posse, of course. The pay was three dollars per day and found; the duty was arduous and often ineffectual. A man with work to do and the will to do it would not ride in such company. The idlers, the drunks, the stupid, or the curious were Simon's fodder.

For a moment Royball Shelly thought he might ride along. The woman, and the man who had stolen his horse—that was almost big enough temptation.

Then he knew he would not, could not. Even discounting his legal status, it would still be a mistake. He had spent years building the personality in which he lived as within a cocoon. He must maintain it at any cost.

He shivered and went into the Chinaman's. He ate a large breakfast. The posse rode out before he had finished.

Chapter 9

THE TEAM was not ill-matched, it was just skittery, Duke thought, and the gelding had a wild eye in harness. The road was smooth enough going north, hardened by the passage of stages, horsemen, and farm wagons. There had been no rain for some time, and he let the reins go loose. The horse and the gelding seemed anxious to get any place where the unfamiliar harness might be shucked. They made good time in the hours between dawn and sunrise.

When the first rays of light struck, the pace slowed a bit, and he saw that Kitty was adjusting to the up and down motion of the buckboard. They had talked very little, intent on the exigencies of the flight.

Now that he could see her in the first fingering of the sun against the sky to the right, he felt warm pity. She was bruised on the left cheek where Avidon had slapped her full-handed, and she was plain dirty. Her clothing was filthy and frayed. Yet her shoulders were held high, and she looked ahead, not back in fear of pursuit.

He said, "I think we can take time to let you change. There's a stream a mile ahead, west of the road."

"Change?"

"I got you some clothing. From Faith Chittley."

She jerked her head toward him. "From Faith?"

"People are funny," he said. "You can't hardly tell about people sometimes."

"Maury ran away. Faith helped you." She shook her bright head, the disarrayed hair flew in the wind.

Duke said, "Maury's been runnin' for years. She got broke up somewhere along the pike. I'd give a heap to know just what it is with Maury."

"I liked her. She was my friend."

"Liked her myself."

"Yes, I know."

He stared straight ahead. Women talked too much, always, but he didn't believe Maury had told everything to this young female. "Knew her in Dodge City."

"Yes, I know."

Duke let it go by, clucking to the horses. The pause for water was a good idea for man and animal, he thought. He could not believe the pursuit was close enough to make it dangerous to stop. He picked the turn-off in his mind, remembering the country in which he was reared, and found it by a cottonwood tree which leaned against the prevailing winds, a tree with a stretching low branch which gave him the shivers—a hanging tree if he ever saw one.

He turned sharply beneath it, pulled up the team, handed the lines to Kitty, got down and found a heavy, broken branch, went back and smeared the track from road to the rear wheels as Kitty walked the team on an angle behind the cottonwoods. He tied the branch to the rear axle, took the lines again, and made for the creek.

The water ran slow and muddy, but it was water. They both drank, then the horses gratefully muzzled the stream. Duke handed Kitty the bundle provided by Faith Chittley. She unwrapped it with deft care and avidly examined the contents.

There was starched underwear, pure white and clean, enough to swelter in when the sun was hot. There was a plain, gingham dress, full-skirted, light blue. That looked as if it had never been worn.

There was a sunbonnet to match the dress. Kitty held it in her hand, turned it over, her eyes widening. "I've never owned one of these in my life."

Duke said, "You better wash up. I'll be watchin' the back trail."

"A sunbonnet," said Kitty. "I'll look like a schoolgirl in these duds."

"You wouldn't call yourself an old-timer, would you?"

Her fair skin suffused with color. She began to answer, sharp, her eyes flashing, then a veil dropped over her natural instinct to strike back. "I guess I've got a lot to learn. I guess you know all about me, Duke."

She started for the creek, handling the new clothing with infinite care, attaching it to the limbs of an alder clump. Duke turned, took the rifle from the back of the buckboard, and plodded up the side of the slope toward the main road.

He had no fear but he was cautious. Any straying band of men down from the Territory might consider a buckboard, a woman, and a man fair game. He cursed again the inability of Kitty to ride. His plans had to be redesigned, thought out.

He heard her call, after awhile, and went back, having seen no sign of human life anywhere. He paused beside the buckboard and rummaged until he found the bundle of cheese and smoked meat Arimendez had provided. He broke it into pieces and turned and waited.

Kitty came into view. She walked with short steps, faltering, like a young girl unsure of herself. He stared.

The years and the experience with Avidon and her skirmish with near-death had been erased as by a miracle. Her cheeks shone with health, were yet hollowed into a beauty enjoyed only by the young. Her eyes were demure, hopeful, a bit bold, challenging, mischievous.

"It fits good," she said.

"The sunbonnet does something to you," he answered without thought. "Nobody'd ever guess"—he broke off, seeing her eyes fill—"Nobody'll suspect we're on the run. You—you could be a bride on her honeymoon."

"With you for the groom?" There was bite in the expression.

He said, for once taken aback, "I'll wash up. There's grub in the buckboard."

He went down to the stream and stripped to the waist. She was a lovely girl, there was no denying it. He cleansed himself to the waist, redonned his slightly used shirt with distaste even though the sun had not yet brought sweat.

She was a desirable girl, and he was tied to her for no one could tell how long. She had more temperament than she needed, which added to the problem. He had no right traipsing around the country with a redhead like Kitty Devlin. Whether people knew him or not—it wasn't proper and right.

He rolled his hat brim, wondering how he could make himself look more the bridegroom, just in case. . . . He put aside the thought. Speed and more speed and some trail-hiding and brains and some luck, that was the way it had to be. He had a half-formed scheme, wild but plausible when he thought of it carefully, allowing for a modicum of luck.

Luck, the gambler's tide of swelling fortune, had always been with him in the pinches, when the odds seemed high against him. No reason to think it had played out.

Kitty was on the seat, chomping away at bread and cheese.

He rehitched the horses and turned them back toward the main road, and Kitty fed him as they rolled along northward. For that time they were in high spirits and without knowledge of the early start which Royball Shelley had given Simon Avidon.

The posse rode helter-skelter. Yank fired off his gun several times before he sobered up, drawing angry yells from men on skittish ponies. Simon Avidon rode at the head of the motley crew. It was a bunch that he would not have cared to lead in pursuit of determined outlaws. It was, however, a crew he could handle in this particular chase. He had to make the best of them.

He had also to keep Donkey under control, which was surprisingly difficult. Duke Parry's cavalier treatment of the deputy had roused a sleeping devil. Hitherto there had been no design, no aim, in Donkey's course of brutal expression of his demon. Now he was beside himself with murderous rage.

He rode beside Avidon, mumbling, "First off he buffaloes me in the Holiday House. Then he cusses me. The way he even looked at me, and him without his gun, when he went in to see the gal—like I was dirt or somethin'."

"Slow down, Donkey. You'll pull the rope on him like I promised. You can put the knot under his ear and pull the rope."

Donkey did not respond with his usual childish glee. "Then he slugs me, I'm asleep, mindin' my own business. You know what, Simon?"

"What?" It was wearisome, but Donkey could not get off the subject, and Avidon knew no way of shutting him up.

"That's the same as shootin' a man in the back. Or a man not wearin' his iron. Ain't it? Hittin' a man in his sleep. Ain't it, Simon?"

"Certainly it is. Stop thinkin' about it and ride." He had Poley Meyer watching the trail. He knew, of course, about the buckboard, the ill-matched harness horses. To overtake a buckboard was no big probem for a mounted posse. Still, he meant to be careful with the Duke. He would not make the error of underestimating the gambler's ingenuity.

"I can pull him up? He don't get no drop, huh, Simon? I can choke him off?"

"Any way you want, Donkey. Now watch for wheel tracks leading off the road, will you?"

Donkey, dedicated, spurred ahead, bending his long nose

toward the side of the road from time to time, mumbling to himself his hymn of hatred.

Sledge and Yankee lagged a bit. Sledge had thought to bring a bottle. They nipped, nursing their morning-after-whim-whams, bemoaning lack of sleep as the cause of their jitters.

"Nothin' wrong with me a drink won't cure," bragged Sledge, wiping his mouth with a dirty cuff.

"First posse I ever rode on," confessed Yank. "Feels kinda funny, chasin' a woman."

"Like what you goin' to do when you catch her?"

"Like I know what's goin' to happen," said Yank. "Gimme another shot of that redeye."

Duke stopped in midmorning at the top of a rise. It was necessary to blow the horses, and there was a tall tree. He dug around in his war bag for the old, folding telescope he had stolen during his days riding dispatch out of Sydney Barracks in the Cheyenne trouble. It was hard, dirty work climbing the tree, but he had to look back along the road. This was his last vantage point for such a survey, he knew.

He steadied himself and adjusted the glass. He closed his left eye and peered.

He almost fell out of the tree. They were not close enough to be identified, but there was no mistaking the cloud of dust; it told the tale by its size and the rapidity with which it soared above the stage road.

He came down very fast and Kitty knew at a glance that things had gone wrong. He climbed into the driver's seat and plucked the buggy whip from its socket.

He said, "I'm about to kill a pair of good enough animals. It hurts me, but that's the way of it. Hang on tight, Kitty."

The team took off. There was a lot of run left in them, at that. He hated to push them this way, but he had in mind the most desperate of his alternate plans, a wild, chancey scheme which was odds-on to fail. There was no other way to go, now.

Avidon must have been discovered before time. Then they had missed the obvious trail he had left at the turn-off to the creek. They were so damned dumb they hadn't even seen the one-way tracks he had left by erasing the ingoing and leaving the outcoming trail—impossible to distinguish without long, skillful examination which way the buckboard had been heading. By their very stupidity they had not paused to lose valuable time.

He drove the horses downgrade. Kitty hung on with both

hands; once, when they twisted in a rut, he thought he was going to lose her.

There was a place he had to reach before the posse topped the rise and might spot them. He had to make the run over ground which was impossible or nearly impossible, but it was his only chance. Traces loose, the horses ran wild.

The buckboard hit the bottom of the grade and immediately there was another slight hill. There was a straight run from its summit and Duke drove on, admiring the horses even as he cracked the light whip.

Kitty said, when the bumping ceased and permitted her to speak, "Are they close?"

"Maybe ten miles. They must've started early and come straight through without thinking. Avidon is smart, all right."

"Have we . . . have we got a chance?"

He grinned, looking straight ahead, wary of an obstruction in the road. "We got guns and shells. We know they're closin' in on us. We know what'd happen if they caught us."

"I can't shoot, neither," she wailed. "I never shot off a gun in my life."

"Don't fret yourself. You can learn quick enough." He might have added that it didn't make any difference, that they couldn't hold off a fully armed posse for any length of time. He would shoot her, he decided, when the time came.

He didn't bother about himself. He knew he could make them kill him. He knew about posses when they have a man cornered, and he knew the Indian way of charging into the guns when the end was inevitable. There wasn't enough nerve in that crew to take him alive if he walked down on them with a gun in each hand.

He drove on. At this speed, he could hold his own until the horses faltered. He whistled a little tune remembered from Dodge City days, a lively jig-time tune.

Kitty was standing it well. Youth and health were on her side. If she was scared, at least she didn't panic. She clung to the stanchion of the wide seat, her sunbonnet tied down tight. If she lived, Kitty would make someone a good wife, he thought.

Time sped beneath the shod feet of the animals. When the first hesitation came to the gelding's pace, Duke slowed them to within the limit of their strength. He was close enough to it, now he thought. Give him an hour. . . .

The hour passed. The sun was high and hot, but there was a slight breeze from the southwest. He began looking for his landmark.

He found it, a red cliff of some proportions. It stood out

like a sore thumb, but there was shale which led to it from a spot twenty feet west of the road.

He took Kitty's soiled clothing to destroy their tracks. The horses stood on the shale, heads down, blowing. Kitty came down and helped, erasing the wheel marks, and hoof-prints. They walked backward, dragging her rumpled, dirty garments behind them. They climbed into the buckboard, sliding a little on the shale, drove on a few rods, and stopped. Duke examined every inch of the ground behind them, could detect no telltale evidence that they had turned here.

He said, "We'll know in awhile. You got to keep your nerve now, Kitty. You see, if we go on, and they do catch onto the trick, they'll nail us in open country. The new trail is yonder, westward. I aim to make it, maybe pick up with a herd, if we're real lucky."

"A trail herd?"

"Headin' for Dodge," he said. "If we're lucky."

"That's if we fool 'em."

He said, picking up the reins, "If we don't fool 'em, Red Cliff over yonder is as good a place as any to make our stand."

She looked toward the promontory. She said, "You mean it's as good a place to die as any, don't you, Duke?"

The horses moved, partially restored but slipping on the loose rock. Duke held the lines tight, steadying them. He said, "Me, I always play out the string. I've seen it run both ways from the middle, I've seen it tough. As yet, here I am. And here you are."

He headed for the safety of the cliff.

Duke had been wrong about one thing. It wasn't stupidity which had brought the posse so quickly up the road. It was because of Poley Meyer.

Poley was sixty. He had been with Carson and Bridger in the mountains, and had known the wild, free days. Then he had come to Holiday, settled in the town, and married. Then, widowed, without children, he had become a great friend of Fitz Warren. He had reached the stage of being unsure of popular enthusiasms.

Poley had not missed the sign of the buckboard. Knowing the country as he did, he had visualized Duke and the girl pausing for water, even for a change of clothing. Poley thought things out, all the way through. He had glimpsed the girl in her cell, noted her dishevelment. He had not approved of this and had mentioned it to Avidon.

When the marshal had ignored him, Poley Meyer had

begun doubting. His grief and anger at Fitz's manner of dying had addled him for awhile, but his feelings were moderated by Duke Parry's actions. Duke had been in to see the girl, had remained aloof from the mob feeling. He remembered Duke's father and his mother, who had also been good friends of him and his wife.

Then Duke took the girl out, and Poley's doubts rose. He talked with Hampton, the smithy, before leaving with the posse, and Hampton had advised him to stay home and mind his business. Hampton was no fool.

Then there was the judge, for whom Poley could have no respect at all. Shelley reminded him of certain Indians he had known who dressed like girls and were tolerated by the tribes in the tongue-clucking, head-shaking way that Indians sometimes adopt toward insane or crippled people.

There was a lot Poley had learned from the Blackfoot and Crow tribes, superior redskins. Their testing of their warriors, while bloodthirsty and fierce, was basically correct. In a tight, you wanted to know who was worthy of trust.

He had never seen the marshal in a real tight, except when Hampton was knocking off the handcuffs after Duke had jumped him and got the girl away. Avidon had come through that all right. Donkey had raved and ranted, but Avidon was cool enough; there was just a twitch in his left cheek, and his eyes were sunken and deadly. He had sense enough to sleep an hour, too, instead of running around. He'd make the trip all right, given another chance at slumber.

The rest of them weren't worth a hoot and a holler. When he saw the wagon track, Poley really thought Duke and the girl were at the creek, sitting ducks for a bunch of hungover bastards. And Avidon; he wouldn't want to see what happened when Avidon closed in. Now, if there was more time, if they overrode Duke and the girl, it would be fairer. So he rode past the sign.

Nobody else saw it. They were all blind and dumb when it came to sign. They were the town, which had only come after the mountain men had walked the steep slopes and deep valleys and made their maps and shown the way to the West. They were the future even more than they were today.

Poley Meyer thought that when he was young he would have given a whoop and led the posse to the fugitives. He would have done this unthinking, because he was the one to find trail and because he wanted to show off what a hi-yu fellow he was. He might have been sick after the hangings, or the shootings, or whatever, and he might even have caught one himself, because Duke would never give up alive; Duke could make them come to him with that easy, quick aim and his ability to make a smart fight.

Poley was beyond that sort of going, now. He needed some time to think about Avidon and Donkey and Yank and Sledge and the others like them. He had to balance things. If Kitty Devlin had killed Fitz, she was for hanging and no two ways about it. Fitz had been a good man. What Poley wanted was a proper court trial. He had come to realize that the only way he could go along with things was to have them chewed over after everyone stopped being mad.

The way he figured it, Duke would know the posse had gone past. Duke would double back and hit west for the trail, no question about it. Then Poley would be able to head him off. It was just a question of thinking it through.

The posse could keep going until the stage stop. There they would learn that Duke had not driven through. Then there would be a milling around and a big hoorah. Avidon would be worried. Poley could go to him quietly and suggest they get rid of Yank and Sledge and Donkey, send them back to check some byways where Duke might have gone. Meantime, Poley would lead the rest of the posse to the new Trail, and they could nab Kitty and Duke before Doan's Store, on the river.

Even if they got into the Territory it would be easy to catch up with them—it wouldn't be the first time a posse had crossed the boundary on a manhunt. It wasn't as if Poley was turning Duke and the gal loose. He couldn't do that, on account of Fitz and his belief in courts of law and all that. He was, he told himself, just putting it off a bit to give the better minds a chance to think, as Poley was thinking.

He couldn't have named you two men with better minds. He couldn't have named one.

He kept on pretending to watch for sign, but he believed Duke was already on the way to the trail. He kept on thinking, trying to imagine Kitty sticking a knife in the back of Fitz Warren and failing. He was building up a lot of trouble and confusion in his mind, doing this.

But he thought he was buying time for it to smooth out. He thought anything was better than Duke being trapped at the creek, where there were plenty of trees with hanging limbs.

Kitty Devlin thought she knew how to squeeze the trigger of the rifle, if need be. She lay against the rock, looking at the sky, which was blue and had never seemed to be such a precious blue, and at the cloud formations, which assumed fantastic shapes.

She asked abruptly, "Did you ever see the ocean?"

"Nope," said Duke. "Just San Francisco Bay. I was drunk at the time." He was watching the road. He thought it pretty near time. The posse should be coming over the rise and down and onto the flats. The red cliff looked like good cover, and they might make a pasear without finding sign. If he were leading the bunch, he would investigate a nice convenient place to fort up like the red cliff.

"Not a bay. The sea. The tides, the moon changes, the way it comes in and in, always and forever. The big, wide ocean, coming in on the sand."

He shrugged. He might get to investigate an ocean some-day. He had been far places, and he would go again, if he lived. "Sounds monotonous."

"That's what I thought. But now, you take the sky up there. It'll be all over everywhere, everything. Bigger than the ocean, because the sky is over all oceans."

"You better pay attention, girl. You better get used to that rifle."

She said, "I'm quick at learning. Don't you worry." She did not turn her attention from the cloud formation which the wind was changing from a charging horse troop into a castle complete with a giant's head. "Living in towns, we never look up at the sky. We look down to watch our step. We look at people, and they look at us." She broke off, lowered her gaze to Duke. "We never do learn about the people. Just look at them. Exchange the time of day. I slept in the same room with Maury. I still don't know why she ran away."

Duke said, "Oceans, skies, women. You pays your money and you takes your choice."

"You keep yourself removed, mostly." She nodded wisely. "You walk apart. It's wonderful if you can do that. I wish I could do that."

She was right, of course. "It's the way a person's made, I reckon."

"But you had to take me out of there."

"Yeah."

"You didn't want to."

"No, I didn't particularly want to."

She seemed satisfied and continued to regard him with her greenish eyes. She was very attractive beneath the sun-bonnet. He looked away to the road.

They were in sight. He put out a hand, and Kitty moved close to him, crouching, although they could stand upright without being seen behind the red rocks. They watched the posse ride, strung out, quieter now then at first, dogged in determination. Avidon looked tall in the lead.

She stared at Avidon. Simon, she had called him, dear Simon, holding him close. She had never loved before, and he had been very dear to her.

The rifle came up in her hands. She felt it pointing itself toward him, as though without her will, aiming at his long, heavy torso that she knew.

Duke took the rifle away from her without looking at her. He held it at trail, watching Poley Meyer.

The veteran was riding with downcast eyes, but loose in the saddle. If he straightened up, Duke thought, if he showed in any way that he saw their sign, the rifle might well be aimed at Avidon and the trigger pulled and the rest of it chanced. Without Avidon, the posse wouldn't be half as dangerous. He lay the barrel along the hot surface of rock and waited.

Kitty whispered in his ear, "Kill him first, Duke."

"No killin'. Not yet," he replied. Poley hadn't made a move. They were going by.

Donkey stopped, stared toward the red cliff. He waved an arm. Avidon spoke sharply to him. Donkey fell into line. The posse went over the horizon and was out of sight.

Chapter 10

THE HORSES were wearying, but they were still full of nerve and possibly fear. Dragging the buckboard over the flat, wild land had spooked them, Duke thought. He headed due west into the afternoon sun, hatbrim low.

Kitty had lapsed into silence. The jarring ride should have exhausted her long before now but she gave gracefully to the motion of the seat, one hand resting on the curved stanchion.

Duke said, "It's only a few more miles, the way I figure."

"But you've never been on the new trail."

"Nope. I was all through with trail drivin' before '76. It's no life for a tender young sprout."

"I believe you."

"A weak mind and a strong back," said Duke. "Take a man wants to live with cattle, own a ranch, live in the saddle, it's all right."

"Or a man who wants a family?"

"That's right."

"But you don't want a family?"

There were more rocks ahead; not mountains, not even foothills, just rugged, rocky country. Privately, Duke wondered about water. There were no trees, no vegetation abounded. It was a desolate piece of country, south of the Red River. If he could find the trail and ride north to Doan's Store, he might have a chance. On the old Chisholm Trail it had been Red River Station, he remembered. He tried to get it placed in his mind, knowing that Red ran north and west from the station.

"You don't want a family?" she persisted.

"Lemme put it this way." He spoke slowly. "Up 'til now the right gal hasn't come along. A man like me, if he settles down, it's in a town. I don't even know a town I like that much. The gal has to be . . . how do I know? How does any man know until it happens?"

She nodded, satisfied. "I see. Guess I thought Simon was the man. Holiday was the town. Sometimes, Duke, you think you know. But it turns out wrong."

"It shouldn't turn out they're goin' to hang you for bein' wrong," he said. There was a general rise to the rocky table-land. He eased the horses on the grade.

She said, "Holiday is your town, Duke. Fitz told me about your family and all."

"Holiday is Avidon's town and the judge's town. Without Fitz, it don't cut it."

She said tentatively, "The Mexican gentleman helped us. And Faith Chittley."

He nodded. "There's others. When something happens like it did, the good people stop and wonder while the bad people do their dirt."

Both horses had their heads down, pulling. It was necessary to weave among the bigger rocks now, heading for the top of the rise. Duke drove with care. Everything was going all right until the rattlesnake rose up almost beneath the legs of the gelding and sounded its warning on the still air.

The Duke was helpless. Bits clenched in their teeth, the horses answered only to the deep, instinctive fear of reptiles which resounded in their small brainpans. They ran as though fresh, far beyond their real powers and endurance.

Checking down on the reins would throw one of them, spilling the buckboard, Duke knew. He held on, feet braced, fists clenched, all his muscles straining. He tried to steer them among the carelessly rolled rocks, knowing they had to wear down on the swelling grade, hoping that they would not founder.

They reached the edge of a gully. There was a treacherous arrangement of small boulders which he tried to avoid. The horses were past obeying the tug of the bit. The left front wheel of the buckboard cracked between the stones.

He felt it go and yelled, "Jump, Kitty!"

She was quick and strong, going over the side and landing on her feet, skidding, staggering, falling into a heap, head up, staring as the team kicked to free themselves of the wreck behind them.

Duke hit on his shoulders, felt a twinge of pain, held onto the reins. When he came up, both horses were down and the gelding had stopped threshing. His own horse made one more effort, then gave up, his right hind leg twisted horribly, his great brown eyes hooded, begging.

Duke looked down at his hands, cramped around the leather of the lines. He straightened out, one finger at a time. He turned his head and saw Kitty rising, limping a little, coming toward him.

He shook his head at her. "Better stay back a minute."

The gelding was already dead. It had probably run out its endurance. He took out his revolver and, without waiting an instant, shot his own horse through the head.

Kitty said, "Oh!"

"Broken leg," said Duke.

"The poor things."

Duke looked at the brow of the hill, then at the buckboard canted brokenly to the left. "Poor us."

He reached down his war bag, the rifle. He rewrapped the bits of food left to them, handed Kitty the half-filled canteen. "Worst of it is, when they do get smart, they'll find all this. You good at walking, Kitty?"

She looked down at her shoes. They were little more than slippers. "Not over rocks."

"We'll have to try it, and quick." He stuffed cartridges into his pockets. "Over that hill."

It looked close, but it was a mile to the summit. They walked, neither of them accustomed to the exercise, over rolling stones, sharp flinty edges. They detoured, picking the smoothest possible path. Duke, sweating, laboring, was glad for Kitty's slow pace.

When they saw the cattle below and the rider on the flank peering up at them, their relief was overwhelming. Kitty almost broke into a run. Here was a smoother slope leading down, there were people. . . .

Duke stopped her. "Here. Take this. It was my mother's, so don't lose it."

She stared at the gold band he had taken from his vest pocket. "Duke! What does this mean?"

"You don't know Texan cattlemen like I do. If they believe we ain't married, anything can happen. Get this straight—we're on our honeymoon. The buckboard broke down; tell the truth about that. They'll send a man to check it and pick up the saddles. They put a big store by saddles, and the judge's is pure fancy."

"You talk like they're . . . foreigners, or something."

"Listen and mind you follow what I say. Don't act too friendly, not any time. Stick within sight of me. Play my hand and be good at it. I aim to get you to Dodge City. Short of there, you ain't safe, Kitty. Remember that. This could be a good thing for us, but I know these Texans. You're a shy bride—don't forget it for a minute."

She said sharply, "I can play the part. Make sure you can."

"Like you said—I'm the groom."

Jack Budington was riding up to them. She twisted the ring on her finger. It was a bit loose. That would be all right, she thought; a swift wedding in Holiday, a hasty purchase of ring, and the excuse for lacking a trousseau. She whispered these details to Duke, and he nodded, putting down the war bags, waiting for Jack Budington to get close enough to palaver.

Duke said, "Howdy. Had a little accident."

"Looks like." Jack was staring at Kitty. His mouth was wide, and the corners twisted up when he smiled, betraying his youth. "Howdy, ma'am."

"I'm Duke Parry, this is my bride, Kitty."

The mouth smoothed out, drooped. Jack still stared at the girl. She wasn't anything that he had pictured. She was short and slim and stood square on her feet, looking back at him with level gaze. She wouldn't be a silent woman, he felt; nor cowlike in her obedience to him. She didn't look like one to draw water and cut wood and mind the house.

She just looked like the woman he wanted. The whole picture rearranged itself. Kitty filled the frame of his dreams, erasing all else.

And she was married. He almost forgot his manners, forgot to offer to fetch their gear. He waved back down to Fairly, indicated the couple on the hilltop, then rode off fast toward the wrecked buckboard. He felt worse than ever.

Duke picked up the war bag and the rifle. He took the canteen from Kitty and strung it over his aching shoulder. She had the pathetic package of bread and cheese in her hand as they started down the hill—nothing else. It looked better that way to Texans, Duke knew. They had peculiar ideas about ladies.

Once Kitty paused, and he turned to look at her. She rested one hand on the sore shoulder and asked in a low, earnest tone, "Duke. You sure you don't want a family?"

He muttered, "It ain't funny," and plowed on down the hill. But it was funny. The red-haired gal had a lot of sand and bottom to be able to pull a remark like that under the circumstances. He began to feel easier in the role they would have to play.

Fairly was not pleased. Nothing which might possibly slow

down the herd for ten minutes was satisfactory to him. On the other hand, he was aware that hospitality was mandatory even to the area in which he found himself. He said grudgingly, "Right sorry 'bout your trouble. Jack and Cooky'll fix you up."

Then he rode away. Jack Budington had brought in the saddles and stowed them in one of the two wagons which carried tools and equipment. From this wagon, Jack dug out a bundle which he unrolled and examined carefully.

He said to Duke, "There's extra blankets. This here tarp'll make a good enough tent for y'all, won't it?"

Duke said, "We can bed down alongside the wagon, if it's all the same to you."

"This'll make it private." The color rose in Jack's unshaven cheeks. "A man wants to be private with his wife."

"Well, thanks," said Duke. There was, he thought, a quality in this young man.

The herd was moving. Jack cut out a pony from the remuda and saddled it. Duke got aboard, but Kitty had to ride one of the wagons. The young cowboy was shocked and amazed when he learned this. He suggested she ride with Cooky. "He's a drunk old coot, but it's better for a lady," he confided to Duke. "You know how some of these waddies are."

"We're putting you to a heap of trouble," said Duke.

"My pleasure." Jack hesitated, then said, "Fairly, he's all foreman. He don't mean anything."

"Probably thinks I'm a town fella," nodded Duke. He sighed. He would have to go to work. "You got some spare gloves?"

Jack glanced at the soft, supple hands, looked again and saw the thick wrists, the muscles between thumbs and forefingers. "Reckon you seen the elephant, Mr. Parry."

"Only one way to prove it."

Jack brought him gloves and a spare reata. He found a white kerchief that would do for a bandanna. The range clothing was all right, although he did not own high-heeled boots for trick riding. He put the pony through a few paces. It was a good enough cutting horse; they certainly would not have given him the best.

No one expected him to work his way. He could have let them believe he was a gambler only, a man of the cities. He would vastly have preferred it that way. Unfortunately, he needed these men.

He had no illusions about Avidon. There would be a reckoning. Flight was impossible now that the buckboard was wrecked. He had only one chance, to make himself a part of the trail drive, to call forth loyalty among the cowboys.

Kitty was already perched on the high seat beside Cooky. Duke rode over and smiled fondly on her. "Are you all right, darlin'?"

She said, "I'm right fine, Dukey."

He winced, tried to cover up his startled resentment at the appellation. Cooky was a red-nosed, thin man with light blue eyes who smelled of alcohol. He sneered down at Duke and slapped the reins at the team drawing the chuck wagon.

Duke rode away, toward the rear of the herd. He knew better than to try and show off his knowledge and skill of the trade. He saw a big man riding drag, taking the dust and pulled in close.

"Where in hell you come from?" the burly man asked, wiping his face with a huge paw.

"Just moseyed in," said Duke. "I'll take it for a spell."

"Fairly say so?" Bull was sulking because Fairly had bawled at him earlier. He blamed Jack Budington, mostly.

Duke said, "He sure ain't goin' to say no."

Bull growled something and rode out of the dust cloud to the point. Fairly saw him, looked back, then rode hard, spoke to Bull, came into the stifling swirl of grit.

"You been up the trail before?" he demanded.

"Not this here one," drawled Duke deliberately.

Fairly stared at him. "Old-timer, eh?"

"Wouldn't say that."

"Well, don't chivvy 'em. I aim to keep every pound on 'em they got."

"Mixed herd," said Duke. "Got to kill the calves?"

"Ain't had too many," said Fairly. "The boys got one in a wagon."

"Anything you say," Duke told him.

The foreman didn't seem too happy, but he rode out of the dust. A hardnose, thought Duke. Nothing would suit him. Fairly hated having a woman along. It might be real hard to get him around on their side; in fact, it might be impossible. Duke knew the breed.

He rode along, hating every grimy minute of it. He had quit this business years ago and had wanted no part of it, not ever. He had sworn that he wouldn't ride with cattle. It took a hell of a circumstance to bring it about, he thought.

That damned Kitty, riding safe and happy on the chuck wagon.

Avidon looked at his watch. They were resting the horses

on the road short ten miles of Red River Station. He said
to Donkey, "Ride in and see if they been through. I don't believe they could have made it."

"They musta made it."

Poley Meyer sat slumped in his saddle, listening. It was
almost time to lead them to the trail. Letting the Duke
and Kitty get clear away wouldn't be right, he had known all
along. Yet he hesitated, stalling, he didn't quite know why.

Avidon said, "We need to rest and think. Your horse is
sound. Swap him for a fresh mount at Red River."

"If they're at the station, what should I do?"

"Get the hell back here quick as you can. No monkey
business. Besides, if Duke sees you first, it'll be your finish,"
said Avidon harshly. "And bring back some supplies."

Donkey took off, dipping his spurs deep into his mount.
Avidon turned to Poley Meyer.

"What do you think?"

"They could've turned off and covered track. It'll take
time and plenty to find the place, if they did."

Avidon nodded grudgingly. "We came too fast to do a
good job of tracking. You reckon they're headed for the
trail?"

"The Duke is canny," said Poley Meyer evasively. "Could
be he headed for the Territory. Could be he got fresh horses
in Red River."

Avidon said, "We'll drift back a ways. Donkey can follow.
Something tells me they turned off."

His intuition was working again. He had not failed to ob-
serve the red cliff. The time element was all wrong. He was
certain the ill-matched horses would not have carried Duke
so swiftly to Red River Station.

The day was waning. They would have to make camp with
what food Donkey could rustle for them, with liquor to
keep them aroused and on the job. Yank and Sledge looked
terrible—they would need sleep. Some of the others were in
just as bad shape, most of them were not hardy in the saddle.

Tomorrow would do just as well, maybe better. He would
make it his business to keep them riled during the camp. He
was good at this, and around the campfire, with a bottle going,
he could tell fond stories of Fitz Warren and his kindness
and goodness and insinuate foulness regarding Kitty and in-
vent calumnies to heap upon Duke Parry, gambler and gun-
slinger.

It was a touchy business, but as the judge said, a man
had to have a goal and aim straight for it. Sitting in the
saddle in the late-afternoon sun, he refused to allow himself

leeway in his thinking. He had started this affair and he would finish it.

Someday, when he was solidly established, he would enjoy the luxury of self-evaluation. In the beginning, of course, in the wild freedom of the frontier, he had seen plainly, only those who were ruthless would succeed. The wild streak of his youth had been extended because he could overlay it with a smile and with good Southern manners and because Judge Shelley had counseled him with wisdom. When he had moments, like the present one, which pressed in on him, lowering his spirits, he looked at the goal ahead and took new heart.

Someday, maybe, in the political arena, he would be able to justify everything. Everything!

Chapter 11

THEY SAT around the fire and listened to the Duke, and Jack Budington watched, alone on the edge of the circle. Al, Jim, Bull, even loudmouth Lefty were all ears at the stories of the boom camps. Fairly was rolled up in his blankets, taking an early nap, and the others were on night duty.

Duke said, "The old trail was a hard enough way to go. This trial is rougher, they say. But Dodge is the queen of trail towns, and at least you get to Dodge."

Lefty said, "Then what? You slick articles trim us at the tables."

Duke reached into a pocket and took out a deck cf cards. Immediately every cowboy present hunched for ward. Lefty said in his rough way, "Chuck some wood on that fire, Jack. What the hell?"

Then he looked at Kitty and stammered, "Beg your pardon, ma'am."

Kitty sat on a blanket at Duke's left. She smiled and answered softly, "I've worked in a saloon, Lefty. I know you don't mean anything."

And coarse, leathery, rasp-tongued Lefty said, "Thank you, ma'am."

Jack went for the wood, angry with himself for lingering on the outskirts. He built up the fire so that they could see the supple hands of the gambler and stood, looking down, not at Duke, but at the woman. She had to be married, of course. It was enough to drive a man loco. She had to be married, had to come over that hill and stand there looking at him and smile that friendly smile and tear him all apart with her damn green eyes. A little girl like her, he would never have believed it could happen.

Now everything was sour. Now he might as well marry Sary and to hell with it.

How could it happen to a man like that? Sure, he was thinking too much of womankind, debating about marrying and all, but never had he thought about a girl like her. She wasn't his kind. Worked in a saloon, she said. He didn't want that sort for mother of his kids. Sure, she married a gambler, what else?

He returned his attention to Duke Parry. Lefty had known about the man, and so had old Cooky, who was all smiles and sweetness and even mostly sober, hanging on every word Duke put out. A gun, a slick tinhorn, that was the kind of man for a saloon girl.

He ate his heart out at the thought of them together.

Duke was showing the faro dealer's tricks. "If you watch his right hand, not the card, you'll know. Most of them can't deal a second unless he shows his middle finger. Like this."

He showed them slow and plain. He did it again and again. Then he winked at them and said, "Some men are just too fast." Then he did it, and they couldn't see the flashing knuckle, they couldn't see anything but a straight deal.

"Not many can do that," said Jim, who was segundo to Fairly for the main owners of the herd. "Masterson ain't that good."

"You're right," said Duke. "He's a good friend of mine and a square-shooter, but he's not a top dealer. Luke Short is the top man."

"Yeah. Luke is best. Square, too."

"The only way to stay healthy and make money is to run a game on the level," said Duke. "It's no good when they know you're crooked. On the other hand, a man has to be on to the tricks or some slicker will take him apart."

He began dealing poker hands. They all sat in, fascinated by the way he made the cards fly around the blanket. He said, "Every gambler has a cold deck or two hid out. These happen to be honest cards. Now, Lefty—you've got three aces."

Lefty said, "Damned if I ain't. . . . Excuse it, ma'am."

Duke went on, "Bull, you've got a four-card high flush. In spades. Al, yours is a full house, eights over sixes. Jim's is an open straight to the king."

He turned over his own hand. He had a four-card straight flush in diamonds to the queen. He gave them their draw, then took one card for himself. They all filled to perfection, but of course the Duke held the winning hand.

"Imagine a pot built from these hands," he said. "Any two-bit sharper can manage it with a cold deck. A few of us can deal it without."

"How can a man tell?" demanded Lefty. "What chance we got?"

"Sharp eyes. A sober man who looks hard can see a tinhorn ring in a cold deck. The telltale knuckle for the second-carder or bottom-dealer. Mainly it's staying off the redeye."

Lefty said, "There goes my pay, right now."

"That's right," said Jim. "Man gets so thirsty on the trail he takes on a load when he hits the first saloon. Then he gets bigger than Shanghai Pierce."

"Nobody's bigger at a table than Shanghai," said Lefty. "He'll bet his last cow."

"Pierce doesn't gamble with tinhorns," said Duke. "I had a go with him, and he knows his poker, believe me."

Duke told about Shanghai Pierce, and Jack Budington didn't listen. He walked away, got more wood for the fire. He managed to stumble over Fairly's feet as he returned to the group. He saw the trail boss twitch in his blankets and raised his voice to ask, "You figure on making it to Doan's Store with us, Mr. Parry?"

Fairly came out of the blankets staring around, angry. His voice blanketed the happy circle around the fire, "What in tarnation's goin' on? Git to bed, you waddies. I won't have no sleepin' in the saddle on this drive!"

They broke up reluctantly. Jack should have felt guilty at depriving them of their fun, but he couldn't stand it any longer. The damn gambler had them mesmerized.

Kitty arose, smiling at one and all, and Duke put his cards away. They went toward the wagon where the tent had been fashioned by willing hands from the tarpaulin Jack had produced.

He found his blankets and dove into them, boots and all. He buried his head. The lousy gambler had her inside that canvas in double harness. He groaned aloud.

He knew then why he had asked the wild question about them going all the way through to Dodge. He couldn't stand it if they did.

Under the canvas it was impossible to stand up straight, yet there was room to maneuver. Kitty watched Duke as he removed his short, sleeveless jacket and folded it with care. Every move he made was sure, she thought. He was a man who always knew exactly what he was doing.

"You sure melted the cowboys," she said.

"I meant to. We might need them bad." He spoke in a low tone, very little more than a whisper. He doffed his boots.

She said, "Can I put out the candle, now?"

"Sure, go ahead."

She blew it out, then snuffed it between her fingers, forgetting the shortage of soap and water. They had given her a basinful, and she had thrown it away after washing her face, but Duke had saved his in a battered bucket, explaining that she might want to rub out some "things." Meaning underwear, she knew. There was nothing for her to wear in Duke's war bag, naturally, and she wondered who would notice first and comment on it.

She said, "We're still in plenty trouble."

"Long as you know," Duke muttered. He was already trying to get comfortable in the soogans, trying not to worry himself out of the sleep he needed. It had been a hard day, and he thought he felt better than he had a right to. He wasn't broken to this kind of life.

She took off her dress and arranged it as best she could. She fumbled with the corselet and the underskirt. If she slept in them, tomorrow would be hideous. She stripped off the stockings, realized Duke could not see her in the darkness. She made up her mind, took off everything, and tried to keep the various articles neat and convenient.

Then she thought about a night wind, or a stampede, or a runaway horse, or any of a number of things which could render her naked on a trail drive. She whimpered a bit at the picture, as though in a nightmare.

"Keep your nerve up," Duke whispered.

It was too late. She had been going on inner courage she hadn't known she possessed for too long. The tears came, and her shoulders shook. In order to keep anyone outside the canvas from hearing, she tried to stifle her sobs in her petticoat. The results were disastrous.

She didn't know Duke was close at hand until she felt him touch her. His voice was in her ear, "I know . . . it's been real rough on you. . . . Try not to let them hear you. We got to play it down the middle with these jaspers, honey."

The kindness, the understanding, the realization of what he had done for her, was doing for her, became too much to bear. She reached out and threw her arms around him. She forgot that she was naked and that Duke was a man. She forgot everything except that she needed reassurance, that someone was offering it to her.

The Duke hadn't had a woman for too long. This one was

young, and it was no time to argue fine points. She demanded of him, and he had never been a man to deny the flesh. He slid down into her blankets, and soon there were two who would not have welcomed the disruption of the cover provided by the tarpaulin.

The dawn was milky when Duke came out of the canvas shelter refreshed, his own man, ready for the roll of the dice. He almost ran into Jack Budington, who did strange things with a water bucket to keep from spilling its contents.

"Hot," said Jack, stammering a little, not looking at Duke. "Thought the missus might . . . you know, women . . . Cooky sent it over."

Duke said, "I can use a dip myself." He rinsed his hands and rubbed his eyes awake. "Kitty'll be plumb happy."

Jack stood there, offering it, and Duke looked closer. The young fellow was paralyzed. His face beneath the beard stubble was crimson. One of those woman-shy kids, with manners, Duke thought.

"Take it to her," he said. "She's anxious to wash out some things, if the wagon can wait."

"It'll wait," said Jack. "Fairly won't like it, but I'll see that it waits."

"Fairly's a good man," said Duke diplomatically. He was foreseeing trouble with Fairly. He went to the picket line and chose a horse he figured wouldn't be prized by one of the riders. He roped it and saddled it and bore its early-morning bucking exercise with patience if not pleasure. He rode to the chuck wagon and accepted scalding liquid which might or might not be coffee.

Cooky said in a whisky voice, "Gamblin' man never can feed in the mornin'."

"Keep something cold for me, Cooky?"

"Mebbe." Cooky had his position to maintain; he was king of the drive, drunk or sober. But he winked at Duke.

Kitty had come out from under the tarp and was accepting the water. He saw her face clearly in the half-light as he rode past. She was looking with great interest and intensity at young Jack Budington.

She was saying, "Well, thank you. I don't want to slow down the drive. Duke explained how important it was to get to Red River before the cattle suffered any."

"You go ahead. This here wagon can catch up."

"No. I think I'll wash the—clothing tomorrow," she said. "I'll use this on me."

He was overwhelmed by her courage, her thoughtfulness

of the herd, everything about her. He said, "Whatever you say, ma'am. Fairly'll be right pleased, I got to admit."

She continued to look at him. One thing she had learned in Holiday, how to estimate a man's feeling regarding her. She could scarcely believe this immediate and complete capitulation, but the message was plain. If she had not been "married" to Duke, she knew, this boy would be bolder. He was shaking with the effort of controlling himself.

"Your name's Jack? Jack Budington?"

"Yes, ma'am. Got a couple hundred cows on this drive. Down home there's a little ranch—free and clear." He couldn't prevent himself from telling her all this. No matter what, he had to make himself known to her, clarify everything about himself. "Just me alone, batchin' it. Goin' to improve my stock with the money from this bunch. It's —it's right interestin', the cattle business."

He was good-looking and young, the right age for her. He owned his own place. He was head over heels, and on sight. She felt deeply the sad stab of ill circumstance. Why did she have to be involved with Duke and trouble just at this time?

She said, "My, that is interesting. I hope we have a chance to talk some more." She remembered in time and added, "Duke will want to hear about it. He talks about investing in a ranch."

Jack swallowed the lie and beamed, then his face fell as he remembered that she was married to Duke. It was all he could do to keep it in mind.

The unlucky pair parted lingeringly and Kitty washed herself, packed the war bag for Duke, tidied up, and had the tarp rolled before the driver had the team ready. The driver was a young lad named Keely, rather stupid but pleasant. She climbed up beside them, and they quickly caught the herd.

A ranch, she thought; a house and some land far from the sea. A young man and the sky overhead and land beneath her feet. she had not hoped for so much, and so should not now be desolated, her sound New England mind told her. When would she toughen to it, to the fate she would suffer because she had left her father and the other eight children and submitted herself to Simon Avidon?

She knew she was doomed. Duke had taken her away from despicable death, but in the end she would pay. She had hoped only to seize a few years' time by escaping Holiday and the noose. Now she had a glimpse through a gate into a garden, and it made things infinitely worse. She saw Jack riding, centaurlike, about his duties, and a tear crept from the corner of her left eye. One tear, that was all she had left, watching Jack Budington in the dust clouds.

Jack was sharp this morning. Not until the sun was high did he cease his vigilance in all parts of the herd and find himself riding beside Fairly.

The trail boss was not talkative this day. Jack reported on a calf born and slaughtered, on this and that, but Fairly only grunted.

Jack said, "Parry is ridin' drag. He's bound to do his part."

Fairly broke silence. "I seen you with the hot water."

Jack stared at him. "So?"

"I seen you look at her."

"I be dam'. What the hell you mean?"

Fairly said, "A jackleg gambler and a piece of calico. On my trail drive. And you suckin' up to them. To her."

Jack said, "I swear, you're plumb loco, Fairly!"

"I seen you. Never a thought of Sary."

"Oh, be goddam," said Jack wildly. "I never heard such talk. I ain't plunked for Sary. That was your doin'."

"Just what I thought," said Fairly coldly. He rode away.

Anger died in a moment. The thing which stuck was that Fairly had noticed him and the way he was with Kitty Parry. Had everyone seen it, then?

Had Kitty noticed?

What about Duke?

He was so beside himself with muddled emotions that he sat slumped on the pony until the wagon caught up with him. He saw Kitty waving at him and started, almost forgetting to answer her friendly gesture.

His mind's eye gave him one glimpse of Sary Fairly, all elbows and knees and clackety tongue. He groaned in abysmal despair. Now the drag was coming up and the dust forced him to use the kerchief. Duke rode up, head lowered, eyed him askance, hauled out long enough to talk through chapped lips.

"How's it going?"

"Uh—all right," said Jack.

"It was plain neighborly to bring Kitty that water."

"A woman's got her needs." Jack blushed, swallowed.

"You married?"

"Hell, no!"

"Don't want to be?"

Jack got a grip on himself. "Duke, if I could find a gal like yours, I'd be married tomorrow."

He dug in the spurs and rode ahead. Duke watched him,

guessing now that Jack had been smitten. It was a loco world, he thought.

And Maury gone again, fleeing her personal ghosts, he thought, adding to the tangled skein. If he could have held Maury, if he had paid her more heed, bolstered her with confidence in her and his own strength, she might not have gone. He had rejected her, with apathy, with carelessness.

He wished he knew where Maury had gone. He might never know, and this would be a bad thing, because in some way Maury complemented him, with her odd fears and behavior.

Maury had not gone far. When Donkey rode into Red River and asked his questions, Maury was in the back of the single, splintery, weather-worn hotel. She was drinking coffee laced with whiskey and listening while Donkey's loud voice raved. She heard the story of Kitty's delivery. She heard of the posse, of the threats against Duke. Now she saw herself caught up again, knew why she had been unable to go farther than Red River Station.

She heard a quiet man's voice say, "Duke Parry, huh? He kilt somebody?"

Donkey explained. His language was obscene.

The quiet man said, "Lady back in yonder. Wouldn't curse so much if I was you."

Donkey came swaying through the door. It was so sudden that she did not have time to prepare herself, but the deputy was too drunk to notice her fear. He peered at her, said, "Maury?"

"Yes," she answered, forcing herself to appear indifferent. "What you doing here, Donkey?"

"You don't know?" He tried to think. "Naw. You left. You don't know 'bout your old pardner, Kitty."

"What about her?" Donkey had mixed it up in his mind. He thought she had left before Kitty was arrested. He was probably the one man from Holiday who was that stupid, thought Maury.

"Kilt old Fitz, that's what she did. Naw . . . I got no time for you. Got to light out. We'll get 'em on the trail. They got to be on the trail. Simon says so, and what Simon don't know, well, it ain't worth knowin'. That's what, sister, and 'member it was me told you."

He went out, walking as if on eggs. She followed, watching him pay the bartender, go out, and mount. He had a pair of sacks suspended across his saddle. He rode southward out of Red River Station.

The quiet voice said, "They got somethin' wrong there. I know the Duke."

It was the bartender, a small, gimpy man named O'Brien. He had brought the whiskey back into the parlor for her. He followed her now, and she allowed him to pour another nip into a fresh cup.

She said, "I know Duke Parry."

"They'll play hell hangin' any gal he yanked outa jail."

"You don't know Simon Avidon."

"Know of him," said the little man. "He ain't the Duke, nor any part of the Duke."

She said, "Then there's Judge Shelley. And all of Holiday."

"Shucks, this feller said Duke took the gal out. Iffen he's got her out, I'll string with Duke."

"Against a posse? Against everybody?"

O'Brien took a long breath, balanced himself on his good leg. "Lady, you don't know Duke real good. You mind to listen about Duke?"

"I'd like to."

"Well, ma'am, I was a dealer once. Worked for Duke. It was up north, Ogallala. Duke always ran a game, once he got his start. Man named Sharpe had the saloon, Duke ran the tables, understand?"

She understood. Duke had operated that way in Dodge.

"Fella came in, name of Carnes. Bucked my faro layout. Kept movin' the chips around, makin' a fuss. Howled down my case keeper. He was a gun-slinger, Carnes."

She nodded. O'Brien's voice was low and steady.

"Got me riled. Now a dealer, he's not supposed to get hot. Supposed to call the boss. Sharpe was there, I coulda called him. But I got smart. I began cheatin' this Carnes. Wanted to make him pay for callin' names and such." He paused, squinted at her. "Carnes caught me. Fired two shots before I could reach for the hide-out gun. Got me in the leg, then Sharpe took his gun away. Now here was the thing, lady: I was wrong. Sharpe said so. Everybody said so. That's the way it goes—get caught and you're wrong. There was no place in Ogallala for me. Duke knew all about it. But he took another stand."

"Yes, I see. Carnes had bucked his game."

"That's it. That's exactly it. Carnes had showed up his game, got me mad, made me make a bad move. I was Duke's man. That's the way Duke seen it."

"And he killed Carnes."

"Not like that, lady," said O'Brien disapprovingly. "He dealt my table until Carnes came in."

"Thereby committing suicide." Yet she saw Duke's justice,

knew the way he thought. She knew an awful lot about him.

"Well, kinda. Carnes tried the same thing. And Duke sure cheated him. Let him know it, then did it to him. Carnes went for his hawgleg. Duke beat him. Then Duke sold out and gimme enough money to come here and buy this bar."

"He did that?"

"I paid him back. But he sure as fire did it."

She thought of this. Then she said, "If they catch Duke on the trail, where would it be? What place?"

He said, "Short of Doan's Store, I reckon. From what that jackass said . . . *if* they catch him."

"They will," she said.

"Then I better saddle up and get my rifle," O'Brien ruminated, looking past her now, out of the window. "I better get down there and look."

She said quickly, "No. It would be no use. There'll be a posse, all bent on killing him . . . and the girl."

He considered this. "I better be there."

"You'll get him killed quicker—and yourself, too," she said. "I've got a better idea."

O'Brien looked helplessly at her. The fire had gone from him years before, she saw. His hands trembled. He had been his own best customer for too many years. At his best he had been a tinhorn, a hapless dealer who got caught. His heart was right, but he wouldn't help the Duke any now, with or without a rifle.

She said, "If he gets away, he'll need help."

"You a good friend of his?"

"Yes," she said. "At least I'm a friend. Goodness has little or nothing to do with it."

"All right," said O'Brien. "I'll wait here—in case."

"Yes, in case," she said. She drained the bitter cup of coffee and whiskey. "Have you got a room for me?"

"Thought you was takin' the next stage north?"

"I thought so, too," she said.

After a moment he said, "Oh. I see. If the Duke comes, you want to be here."

"What I want also has nothing to do with it." She went toward the stairs leading up to the rooms. "I just can't run any more. I'm tired. I never knew how utterly weary I was until I got on that stage. I never knew."

She went up the stairs, her legs like lead. She felt numb all over as she loosened her clothing, lay upon the narrow, hard bed, none too clean, which was the best Red River Station offered.

98   William R. Cox

There was no reason for anything, she thought. Avidon would catch up with Duke and kill him.

She got up and fumbled in her carpetbag. She found the bottle of laudanum. She put it on the bare dresser beside a pitcher of brackish water.

She went back and lay on her side, her legs curled up, one hand under her cheek; she stared at the blue of the bottle and knew she was doomed.

Chapter 12

THE MORNING was bright, and Simon Avidon felt refreshed and alive and strong. The nightmarish dreams of last night were a half-memory; his mind was in command and working like a machine. All doubts were resolved: today he would hang the woman and shoot the Duke, or have him shot.

They had encamped near the red cliff. Donkey told about seeing Maury and about O'Brien and the certainty that the fugitives couldn't possibly have reached Red River Station. The boys had drunk it up, and now they were boozy, woozy, and cantankerous, without coffee due to Donkey's witlessness, searching last night's dead soldiers for sips of whiskey to get them going.

They would be in a murderous mood, thought Avidon. Only Poley Meyer and Soapy Simms, who had abstained in most part, seemed in any kind of condition.

Avidon said to Poley, "What do you think?"

"There's some scratches here and there." Poley gestured at the shale. "Could be they went this way."

"Plenty of drives going up the trail. Duke figures to pick up with someone he knows, or who knows him."

"Could be."

Soapy Simms said, "Duke drove the old trail. Plenty folks know him."

There was something in the eye of Poley Meyer which struck at Avidon's sensitivity. He was sharp this morning, he congratulated himself. If Poley could detect tracks or anything suspiciously like tracks this morning, why not yesterday?

He said tentatively, "Might be trouble ahead. Those trail drivers are plenty tough."

He thought Poley brightened. Soapy considered, then said, "I'm a cattleman myself. I been up and down and around. I can talk to them waddies any old time."

Poley turned his head away. Inspiration came to Avidon. He spelled it out slowly. "Still, might be well to have everything legal. We don't want a war with cowboys or anybody else. This has got to be right." He paused, then said sharply, "Poley, I got an idea. You ride back to town. Get Judge Shelley."

"What in tarnation for?" Poley's eyes widened.

"Tell him to bring any papers necessary to arrest Duke Parry. Tell him what we might be up against. You can track us to where we pick them up. You're the only one can be sure of that."

Poley said, "It's kind of funny, doin' it that way, Simon. Like you're scared, or something."

"I'm scared of one of us getting killed," said Avidon solemnly. "Look, Poley, we don't need you now. We cut to the trail and anybody can find buckboard tracks. We just keep riding 'til we find them, that's all."

Soapy added, "Slow as a drive goes, we oughta have 'em by noon. If we're lucky."

"Noon?" Poley squinted at the early sun. "Yeah, reckon you can, at that." He didn't want Duke to get away, he reminded himself. This was a chance to avoid the final issue, the one his mind kept ducking away from. "Yeah. O.K."

Avidon watched the old-timer ride southward. Poley would maybe come back with the judge, possibly not. The plot was working as it had the day Fitz . . . got killed. His mind conceived these bits and pieces without struggle. No use to deny it, he had a genius for politics.

He yelled to the men. They mounted and followed him. Soapy now rode in the van. He was the second best tracker.

Donkey was nursing his venom along with the bile which whiskey had raised in his throat. Under his breath he cursed a steady stream, conveying to some others that the whole thing, including today's headache, was the fault of Duke Parry.

Yank was unsteady in the saddle, Sledge scarcely aware of the time and place. They were all suffering from overindulgence and lack of accustomed sleep in whatever shoddy beds.

The horses slipped on the shale and the sun mounted high. Soapy found the trail of the buckboard, and then they saw the wreck and the dead team. Avidon rode close, looking down at the judge's gelding, and said, "There'll be hell to pay over this."

Soapy sniffed. "Dam' show hoss never was no good."

"Duke took the saddles. So, he picked up with somebody."

"Plenty of trail drives goin' up to Dodge."

"Like you said," Avidon suggested, "We'll talk to them when we catch up."

"They'll give in to the law."

"You calm them down. I'll do the rest."

Donkey crowded his pony forward. "We're goin' to hang Duke Parry. You said we could."

"Got to get him away from everybody," said Avidon soothingly. "This is a private party."

"Just so's we hang him."

They rode on, at a moderate pace, because the prey was in easy distance now, and Avidon wanted to save the horses. He was thinking of the girl. They had to hang the girl. He must talk Shelley into it. If they strung up Duke, the girl had to go with him.

The wheels went around in his mind. Maybe he had made a mistake sending for the judge. Maybe it would have been better to shoot the two of them for trying to escape.

No, he thought, there might be someone on the posse who would feel remorseful and talk. With the judge on hand, they could make it legal, somehow or other. Hanging was solemn, a community act that would involve them all, so that no one of them could renege in the future.

There would be those who cried lynch law, but weren't there always?

He had been right. It was his day to be right. The Texan trail drivers would listen. There would be no problem. Kitty and the Duke would not see sunset today.

Duke looked at the morning sun and wondered how soon the posse would catch up. He ate his sandwich, thick bread and cold meat, and talked a moment with Kitty.

She said, "Duke—what's the matter with me?"

"Nothing. Not a thing."

Her eyes were sorrowful. "I threw myself at you. Am I bad, Duke? Am I wicked?"

"No, Kitty. You're normal," he said. He couldn't point out to her that she had been sleeping with Avidon, that she had missed having a man. There were no words in him to explain, so he changed the subject. "They're going to catch up with us, you know."

"Are you sure?" Fear banished other emotions from her.

"I've known it right along. Thought I could get this crowd with us."

"That nice boy, Jack, he'll be with us."

"Maybe. The others are all right, except the boss. For some reason I can't get to Fairly."

"You . . . you want me to try? Be nice to him?"

"We'll both try tonight . . . if it goes that long."

"You think they might catch up today?"

"Could be. Remember to keep quiet and leave everything to me. These trail drivers like a show of gameness."

"I'll try, Duke. But I'm awful scared."

"Just don't show it."

"I'll try."

It was all he could expect from her. He rode back to the dusty tail of the slow-walking cattle. Fairly wasn't going to lose an ounce off them if he could help it. If the buckboard hadn't broken down there would have been a chance to get out ahead and . . .

He broke off. Sooner or later, mounted men could catch a wagon. Sooner or later, in Texas or in the Territory. Maybe they were better off with this crowd.

He saw Jack Budington ride to the wagon and begin talking to Kitty. She was smiling and dimpling and doing her best to make a friend of him. Too bad it wasn't Fairly instead of Budington.

Fairly came racing down on a hammerheaded dun pony and hollered, "Parry, if you're gonna ride drag, get them animals up."

Then he rode back and yelled something at Jack, who touched his sombrero brim at Kitty and followed the trail boss.

There was something here that Duke could not understand. Fairly had plain taken a dislike to them. They were not hampering the drive; indeed, Duke was working as hard as anyone, and Kitty was merely taking up room on a seat which would have been empty.

His pony pulled up lame just before noon. He spoke to Fairly, who grunted at him as though it were his fault. Then Jack Budington offered the use of a black in his string, a really fine animal, and Duke was grateful. But it only seemed to enrage Fairly further.

Duke was riding out of the dust for a moment when the posse came down off the hills to the trail.

For the first time in his grown life he felt the distinct urge to run away.

It shocked him, held him to the dust cloud of the herd's tail end. He examined it, realizing that he had never been in such a tight before, not even close to one. He had a good horse under him, he might ride up the lee side of the herd and get a start before Avidon saw him. He might get to Doan's Store—or to Red River Station, where a man named O'Brien owed him a favor.

All these thoughts fled through his mind in a second. Then he was clear of it.

He saw Fairly rein in and wait, and he saw Avidon unerringly recognize the big man as the trail boss and go to him. He rode out of the concealing cloud of alkali and ran the pony swiftly to the wagon. Keeley was looking off, interested, not alarmed or perturbed.

Kitty said, "So soon, Duke? So soon?"

The driver scowled, staring at them. "This you folks's trouble?"

"In spades," said Duke. "Stay tight, Kitty."

The boy said, "Nobody's gonna bother Miss Kitty while I'm around." He hauled a rifle from under the seat. "What's it all about, anyhow?"

"Tell him," Duke said to Kitty. Then he rode toward Avidon and Fairly, shifting his pistol pocket so that it hung within reach, loosening his rifle in the scabbard. It was, he knew, going to be touch and go. He saw Jack Budington heading in toward them. The drive slowed down, stopped, as Bull, Lefty, and Al raced to the possible defense of the trail boss.

Fairly was thunder-browed. "Duke Parry? These here men want you."

"Is that so?" Duke reined in the black pony.

"They say you ain't married no way to that woman."

"They're right about that," said Duke apologetically. "You can see how it was."

Jack Budington was just within his range of vision. He saw the blank expression, the immediate radiance which succeeded, saw Jack reach for his rifle butt. He stuck this observation in the background of his mind even as he paid strict attention to Avidon and the posse, and to Fairly. It all depended upon the trail boss.

Fairly said with the first note of doubt, "She—the woman —they want her for murder?"

"Murder before witnesses," Avidon said in a ringing voice.

"One alleged witness," said Duke, matching the marshal's loud clarity. He picked out Donkey, pointed to him. "That hangdog, yella critter."

Donkey's eyes glittered, staring at Duke. His hand shook,

moving to his revolver, then shied away, rested on the pommel of the saddle, still trembling. His face was set in rigid lines of hatred.

Avidon tried to go on, but Duke overrode him. "They framed Kitty Devlin for a noose. I took her away. That's the story, the whole story."

Fairly interrupted, still chewing at the thought uppermost in his slow mind. "You and her—she ain't your woman nohow?"

"She's a girl who needs help," snapped Duke. "You turn her over to this crowd, and she'll be hanged before night."

Jack Budington's rifle crept out of the boot and was across his saddle. He said harshly, "Nobody's hangin' no woman no time."

Fairly said, "Now, wait a minute." He eyed Jack askance. "No use startin' an uproar."

"You heard Duke. He said they'd hang her."

"Let's listen to the lawman. This here is a posse, not a gang. They carry papers, Jack."

"I don't give a dam' if they carry cannons. They ain't going to hang Kit . . . any woman. Not while I'm alive."

Duke let the cowman carry the ball. He was puzzled to his shoes about Fairly. He had thought he could rouse them all by a flat assertion that Kitty was in danger of hanging. Ordinarily he could have depended upon the instant reaction of these men. The trail boss was bucking him for no apparent reason.

Avidon stepped into the argument. "Believe me, Mr. Fairly, Parry is trying to stampede you. We merely want the woman for murder. We want Parry for breaking her out of jail, for horse stealing."

Fairly looked at Duke. "You stole a hoss, too?"

"And a buckboard," said Duke pleasantly. "I'll be glad to pay for them. You see, we couldn't use the stage, and no trains run from Holiday."

"You stole a hoss," said Fairly accusingly, stubbornly.

Again Avidon was ready. "He beat up on Donkey and me. He took Judge Shelley's silver-plated saddle—reckon he must have it with him."

The boy on the wagon tossed a blanket over the saddle, but looked worried. Kitty spoke to him. She was calm as a clear day on the sea of which she had spoken.

Donkey could no longer restrain himself. "He buffaloed me! Stole our irons and put 'em on us. Left us layin' there all night. He hit me when I was asleep."

Duke said, "I hit him awake when he was layin' for me. I hit him asleep. I haven't shot him, not yet."

"There'll be no shootin'," said Fairly darkly. He assured himself that his men were behind him, spread out in proper fashion, facing the posse, jealous of the terrain, suspicious of lawmen. "I'll settle this."

"Correct, Mr. Fairly," said Avidon agreeably. "All we want is to execute our warrants of arrest."

"All you want is to execute Kitty," corrected Duke.

"Arrest her," said Avidon, not looking at Duke. "To be taken back to Holiday and tried in Judge Royball Shelley's court of law. All legal and right, Mr. Fairly."

Jack Budington muttered, "I be damned if it's right. Murder?" He raised his voice, "What murder? I'd like to know."

Avidon started the story, his version. Duke cut in, "But Avidon was there, and his Donkey. And the knife—Kitty had lost the knife."

"That remains to be proven in court," said Avidon. He was holding his temper perfectly. If Duke missed a beat, the calmness and cheerfulness of Avidon would tip the scales.

Jack said positively, "I don't believe she killed him."

"Neither do I," said Duke. "But the town believes it. The town sent out this shoddy bunch to get us and see that we are never tried. Look at them! Look at Mr. Avidon's posse. Still half-drunk, itching to get back to town and celebrate a lynching!"

Fairly looked. He was a man who essayed to do the right thing. He hated the thought of Kitty unmarried and Jack Budington casting calf's eyes at her and poor Sary ready for mating. But he wanted things the way they should be, fitting and proper.

Jack looked. His finger curled around the trigger of the rifle.

The driver looked and motioned with his gun muzzle. Lefty and Al and Bull looked and spat tobacco juice and snorted through their noses. Fairly didn't miss the signs.

Duke said calmly, "I want to get Kitty where she can have a real trial. Not in Holiday. In Austin, maybe. But she won't live to make it if you turn us over to Avidon."

"You can't obstruct justice on the word of a man like Duke Parry," Avidon argued. "This is Texas, and I'm an officer. All I ask is to make my arrest."

Fairly was weakening. Avidon's confidence was having its effect. Duke cocked the rifle, held it in his left hand. He could get out the revolver and shoot several of them, he knew.

Donkey howled, "Anyways, who's gonna stop us? We got rights. We're takin' 'em, and if we want to hang 'em, that's our dam' business."

Duke sighed with relief. He eased off the hammer of the rifle, put it away. He let Jack Budington handle it, backing off the black horse a step or two, giving himself and Jack room.

"By God if it is!" Jack shouted. "Al, Lefty, Bull? You with me?"

They growled in their throats. Fairly, tilting his head toward Donkey, said, "Marshal, your man's got a big mouth."

Donkey rode forth, his right fist clenched. "This here is agin' the law of Texas. That cussed Duke Parry deserves hangin', and I'm the very one to do it."

Duke saw that there was clear space between them. He said softly, "Donkey."

Beside himself with fury, the man wheeled to face him. "I'll choke you with hemp, by God!"

Duke said, "No, Donkey. Because now I can't let you have the chance."

"Now, just a minute," Avidon said sharply. He tried to spur forward, but Soapy held him back, whispering. Avidon's nostrils pinched white. He fought for control.

Fairly and the others gave ground, leaving Donkey alone on his horse, five yards from Duke and the black.

It was chancey, Duke knew. There were two sides to it. However, he figured Fairly might make his decision against them. Avidon was, after all, what he said, the law. The present consideration was that, in the eyes of Texas cowmen, Duke had been threatened and was honorbound to make a play.

He said, "You better go for something, Donkey. A gun—maybe that knife you like to use?"

Donkey said, "Damn you, damn you!"

He went for the revolver. Duke let him get it out, aim it. He checked the black pony. Donkey fired.

The shot missed, and Donkey fired again.

Duke felt the wind of that one. He took the pistol from his pocket and fired offhand, seemingly without aim.

Donkey went over backward, twisted, slid down, his foot caught in the stirrup. Fairly reached the horse first and prevented the deputy from being dragged.

Duke reloaded the empty chamber of his gun. He said quietly, "If y'all turn us over and I get hanged, it won't be by that coyote. A man's got his pride."

Jack Budington said fiercely, "Nobody's goin' to turn you over."

Fairly was looking down at Donkey, shot through the heart, dead as a doornail. "Now, I dunno. Look at the herd, standin', and us headin' for water we need. I got no time for this. The marshal's got warrants. It's the law."

"Since when do we care for town law?" said Jack. "Duke says Mrs. . . . the gal . . . ain't guilty. Why should he go to all the trouble to take her out if she's guilty? The Duke ain't no dummy."

"Yeah," said Lefty. "The Duke's plain smart."

He was the first of the men to say a word. Fairly looked reproachfully at him, then to the others. They all nodded confirmation. The Duke was too clever to make a dumb play, they agreed.

Fairly hesitated. He said, "Well." He looked at Avidon. He said, "You see how it is?"

"We don't want a fight with your men," said Avidon.

"Well, then?"

Avidon drew a deep breath. "Can you lend us a shovel?"

Al wheeled and went to the wagon where Kitty sat. He looked up at her, winked. He took a shovel from the driver and brought it back.

Avidon said, "We'll bury Donkey."

"Sure," said Fairly, relieved. "Come on, you highbinders. Get them cattle movin'. Hiya! Get along there!"

They rode toward the herd in a cloud of dust, Duke among them.

But it wasn't finished, Duke knew. It wasn't even close to the end. Avidon had been too ready to parley, to accept defeat. There was another act to come.

He paused to speak to Kitty.

She said, "I'm glad you killed Donkey. I didn't ever believe I'd be glad about anybody dyin'. But now I feel glad."

"Jack would have started a shoot-out right here if I didn't," said Duke. "You know they'll stick with it, don't you?"

"Yes. They won't go back without us. What can I do, Duke?"

"Be your pert self," said Duke. "Be extra nice to Jack."

He saw her blush, and then Jack was coming toward them. He detected the new glint in Jack's eyes, the swagger in the saddle, the obliviousness to anything but Kitty high upon the seat of the wagon. He hastily withdrew, his mind turning over what might come to happen, the spot reserved for Jack and his intentions now free.

What do you know? he thought. Smack out here on the trail, Kitty meets the Man.

Now, if she could stay alive, maybe the kid would have a chance after all.

He fell back into his position in the drag. He thought hard about Avidon and the posse and about Kitty and the way Jack had exploded every time mention was made of her arrest, and about what might happen and about his own position.

He fell farther and farther back, hidden from the others by the dust.

Chapter 13

ROYBALL SHELLEY felt the tears on his cheeks. He could not prevent them; they rolled down and dropped on his folded hands. The corpse of the gelding was already swollen and ugly, but he could only see it proud and shining, bearing him boldly through the street for all to admire.

Poley Meyer, lectured on the strict pursuance of the law for miles of riding, stood by and sympathized. The judge had set a heap of store by that horse, more than seemed fitting.

Shelley found his voice. "The man who committed this deed is a monster! He stole, he killed. He shall be punished to the full extent of the law! The full extent, I say."

Poley Meyer said, "Yep. Well, reckon they got him by now. You want to go along, Judge?"

To make things worse, there had been only a tough and bony hack left in the livery stable for Shelley to ride. The beast had a shambling gait which ate up space but was hard on the rider. They mounted and went on down toward the trail.

To their surprise, they found the posse camped, sitting around, disorganized. When they rode in, Avidon came to them and said, "We've been hoping you'd be along about now. There's a problem, Judge."

"You haven't located them?"

"Oh, we found them, all right. In the middle of a tough bunch of trail drivers who don't want to give them up."

The judge caught sight of a fresh mound of earth with the shovel still stuck into it. He looked around, counting noses. "Donkey?"

Avidon nodded. "Parry gave him two free shots. Donkey was out of his mind mad. He missed."

"Another killing. This man, I tell you, has gone beyond all reason."

"Duke gave Donkey the first two shots," said Avidon patiently.

"Aware that Donkey, in his state of mind, could not hit him," said Shelley flatly. "Parry is, I repeat, a monster in human form."

Avidon remembered the dead gelding, the stolen saddle. He said, "Why, sure, Judge. Only you can't charge him on Donkey's killin'. We got enough on him. Horse stealin' is enough to hang a man in this state. Only thing is, we've got to get him and the gal away from the trail drivers."

Shelley's back was stiff and straight. "Those men are Texans. They must be forced to respect Texas law."

"That's just it."

"If need be, we will use arms against them."

Avidon said easily, "Now, Judge, think a minute. Let's look at it plain and figure it out. There's plenty of guns among those trail drivers. They know how to use 'em. We go in there shootin' and there'll be dead men all over the countryside."

Yank and Sledge moved restlessly. Several others murmured. Judge Shelley glared at them, then at Avidon.

"You have every right to ambush them. Call upon them to surrender the fugitives. If they refuse—cut them down."

"You ever tried to bushwhack a bunch strung out around a herd of cattle? Listen to reason, Judge. We've got to have a plan, a smart strategy."

The dead horse had been the symbol of his manhood, Royball Shelley realized. He must recapture something which was missing from him. He moved away, and Avidon followed.

Avidon said in low tones, "This is no bunch to fight with Texas cowmen, Judge. A hangin', sure, they're up to it. Maybe a couple of them like Poley and Soapy Simms are serious and game. That's all. The rest are nothin'."

"My saddle," muttered Shelley. "Didn't even leave me the saddle."

"Pull yourself together. We've got to decide when, where, and how to hit them."

"The law," droned the judge. "The law will take care of them."

"We're the law, remember?"

"Yes. That is correct." He shook himself. The fuzzy edges vanished from his mind. "I am not a fighter, Simon. Haven't you any ideas?"

"The trail boss, Fairly, is willing to give them up. There's a wild young waddy against us. We've got to go in and try them again, and you'll have to go up front."

"On that nag?" Shelley shuddered. "No dignity, man! The law must come cloaked in dignity."

"You can take my horse," said Avidon. "Just so you show authority. Maybe they won't go against a judge."

"Yes. You are right," said Shelley. "They dare not refuse to give up fugitives from the law."

Simon Avidon sighed. He gave Shelley a leg up on his mount. He bestrode the livery stable hack. At least he had the judge in motion. Duke had shaken his confidence with the bullet that killed Donkey. If only the fool deputy hadn't missed . . . but Avidon was student enough to realize that his own weakness was in the deputy he had hired. "No chain is stronger than its weakest link," he repeated from the old copybook he had conned in Savannah.

A whiff of the heated air from the plain came to him, reminding him of Georgia on a similar day, and for an instant his mind split and he wondered with empty middle what he was doing here, in Texas, intent on hanging a woman and killing a man. He threw it off with a hard shake of his head.

He had to plan, to think of some way to make Fairly go along with him and turn over Kitty and the Duke. The judge might just do it, swing the balance his way. If only some unexpected turn of events would lend help. . . .

The Duke arose from his hiding place among the red rocks and rubbed his sore knees. He plodded back toward the place in the shadow of the red cliffs where he had left Jack Budington's good black pony.

The arrival of the judge had set a train of thought to chugging in his mind. He estimated Fairly as being on the fence despite Donkey's outburst. He believed that the trail boss could control his men, except Jack. He imagined that Fairly would tie Jack up if need be.

Between them, Shelley and Avidon could easily convince the cowboys that the law must prevail. Threats of holding the herd at Doan's Store would be enough to send Fairly berserk.

Again he estimated time, wondering if he had a chance to do anything at all. His vague plan had no substance and depended far too much upon chance.

Lady Luck, he thought, you've always been good to me. Now I'm asking a whole hell of a lot too much. But, you see, this is a matter of the honor of Duke Parry. One more time, he pleaded, just one more time.

He got on the pony and said, "You seem like a good one. I hope you are. You're carrying what might be a couple lives, might be a lot of lives."

He rode.

Upon inspiration, Avidon decided that he and the judge would go in alone. For insurance he organized two separate details of the posse and put Soapy Simms in charge of one and Poley Meyer at the head of the other. He had some doubt about Soapy as well as Poley, and thus kept them separated.

The judge had regained full control of himself. He rode up to Fairly and stared at him with bleak eyes.

Fairly said loudly, "Now, by damn, this is too much. I got to get these animals to water."

"Sir, you have first to satisfy the law of your state," intoned the judge in his best courtroom voice.

"We been through all that," complained Fairly. "If you got somethin' to say, spit it out fast."

"I am Judge Royball Shelley, in whose jurisdiction the crime of murder occurred. I am empowered to hold court, pronounce judgment. I call upon you to deliver one woman, namely Kitty Devlin, accused of murder. I further demand the person of Duke Parry, horse thief. I have full papers, issued by me, which you have refused to honor upon demand of Marshal Avidon."

The men had pulled in, wary, bunched behind Fairly. Jack Budington flew straight to the wagon. The judge's speech sounded awesome to untutored ears. The law was beginning to mean something in Texas, after all.

Fairly yelled, "Duke Parry! Come on up here and answer this here judge."

The dust cloud was settling in the rear. Everyone looked for Duke to come out of it.

Jack said, disbelieving, "Why—he ain't back yonder."

Kitty's eyes ached with staring, searching. "Oh, no!"

"He's—he's done run out."

"He couldn't have. He couldn't do it," she wept.

"He ain't there." Jack thumbed back the hammer of his Winchester. "I won't let 'em take you, Miss Kitty. I swear I won't."

"But the Duke. I'm alone, now that he's gone. Don't you see? He was the only one that believed."

"I believe."

"You weren't there." She dried her tears. She had to get

back her nerve. She said gently, "Don't get hurt tryin' to help me. It's no use, if Duke is gone."

"They can't do it," he said. "They'll have to kill me first."

"They'll do that, too," she said. The first trees, signifying that the river was not far ahead, loomed in the distance. She looked away from them. She saw a rope at Avidon's saddle. It fascinated her. One hand crept to her neck.

"They won't," said Jack Budington. "I . . . I got other plans for you and me, Miss Kitty."

She looked at him and already he seemed far away, a dim figure as though on another planet.

Avidon said courteously, "Mr. Fairly, the Duke has realized the uselessness of all this palaver. He's run off to save his own hide. This alone proves the woman guilty."

Fairly squirmed, fumed. "This here is a trail drive, not a picnic. I didn't ask for nobody to join us. All I want is to get them cattle to water."

Jack Budington rode in close, but not too close. "You ain't goin' to turn her over."

Fairly turned, saw the menacing muzzle of the rifle. "Now, Jack, you hold on."

Bull was scowling. "Yeah, Jack, if Duke run out, why should we fight a posse?"

Lefty and Al and Fairly, Jack saw at once, were against him. Keely, Cooky, and maybe a couple of other hands were within earshot. He cast around for a solution.

He said, "It don't prove Kitty Devlin killed anybody."

"The boy's right," called Cooky.

Avidon wished he had brought in his men, now. A sudden move against Jack Budington might do it. Then he realized that the boy on the wagon had his rifle ready and that Cooky was packing a wicked-looking old Frontier Colt .45.

Judge Shelley repeated, "The law is supreme. This is a matter for the courts."

Avidon breathed a sudden gulp of air. He said, "Now, just a minute. The judge is right. You agree?"

"If the law is fair," said Jack.

"All right." Avidon was excited. "Judge, will you hold court right here?"

Mouths went agape. The men looked at one another, at the lean, straight-backed Shelley. To them in that moment he suddenly seemed the embodiment of all courts, all justice.

"I will," said the judge.

"My herd," said Fairly. "I got to get to water."

"Send it on. We'll impound a jury from your men and the posse, even Stephen. The rest can chivvy the herd along to water," said Avidon, his mind flowing full. "Right, Judge?"

"Where I sit, there is the court of law," pronounced Shelley solemnly.

"No!" cried Jack. "It ain't right."

"It's right and square," said Fairly. "You can't sit on no jury, neither. You've already made up your mind."

"Choose among the others," said Avidon carelessly. "Any twelve men will do. We know our case."

His blood ran hot with the implications. Once tried and condemned and the verdict written down, the hanging would follow at discretion. That is, they could stretch the girl to yonder trees and be done with it. There might be some slight criticism, but Judge Shelley's presence would legalize everything.

He congratulated himself, picking Yank, Sledge, four other nitwits to serve on the jury, finding Poley and Soapy and admonishing them to watch the herd and make sure there was no shenanigans by Jack Budington, Keely, or Cooky.

Jack had retreated to Kitty's side. He said, "I won't leave. I'll be nearby. Don't you fret."

She said, "Why, Jack, it's monstrous nice of you. But you can see that without Duke I've no chance. They mean to hang me before dark."

"I'll kill a-plenty of them first," he said.

"And die yourself? It's no use, Jack."

He gazed at her, his heart in his eyes. "I'd consider it no more'n right, Kitty, to die with you."

"Maybe—maybe you can shoot before they hang me?"

"It'll never come to that. You mark my words. I'll see to it. Cooky and Keely are with me."

"They've set up a court. It'll be legal in everyone's eyes. They'll tell their lies. It was my knife in Fitz's back, I never denied it. Simon will repeat what Donkey said, that Donkey saw me. You see, it's no good," she told him. "Don't get killed, Jack. If you can save me from the strangling, that'll be enough."

"I'll take some with us," he promised. The truth of her words were closing in on him, stripping him of belief. "I'll take Avidon and some others."

"If they let you." She smiled thinly, hearing them call her name, reaching for his hand to help her down from the wagon. His grip nearly broke her fingers, but she smiled at him and saw that his heart was very near to breaking, then. It helped her.

He got down from the horse and walked toward the waiting group. It was the most incongruous court ever assembled.

Judge Shelley had dismounted and was standing alone. The twelve men were huddled, shifting their weight from foot to foot, uncomfortable, but intrigued with their own importance. Fairly stood to one side.

Avidon motioned peremptorily to a spot alone where Kitty should take her place. As Jack moved with her, he felt the sudden pressure of a revolver muzzle in his ribs.

The marshal said sharply, "Fairly, this man has no right to stand guard over the prisoner with a loaded rifle."

Fairly hesitated just one instant, then he nodded. Before Jack could make a move he was stripped of his weapon and nudged to a position beside Fairly.

He yelled, "I be damned if you do," and swung at Avidon.

Avidon hit him alongside the head with the barrel of his revolver. He said hotly, "Is this the way you allow your men to act in a court of law, Fairly?"

The trail boss blinked, said slowly, "Well, no." He looked down at the unconscious Jack. "He'll be quiet for awhile."

In the background Cooky and Keely were covered by several guns. Fairly looked to see that the herd was already moving northward. He said grimly, "Get on with it."

The judge said in sepulchral tones, "This court of law is now in session. We will hear the first witness."

All the time Simon Avidon was swearing her life away, Kitty looked at the prone body of Jack Budington, oblivious. When he stirred, they tied him with a reata, and she lost all hope.

Duke got down off the lathered black pony and decided the horse still had run in him if he cooled off right. There was the usual small boy lurking nearby, and he gave him a dollar to walk the animal and rub him down with straw.

Inside the hotel bar he felt limp, and when O'Brien yelled, "I knew it! I knew you'd get away," he paid no immediate attention, drinking the instantly proffered whiskey.

He asked, "O'Brien, is Hoss Safford still marshal here?"

"Sure he is. Tell me about it, Duke. What happened?"

"I've got to see Hoss, right away."

O'Brien shook his head. "He ain't here. Him and his deputy rode out on some business about a bunch of cattle some galoots took from Old Man Healy."

Duke put his head down on the bar. He heard dimly the quiet voice of O'Brien, "She said you was done for, but I knew better. I'd 've been out there with a gun tryin' to find you if she hadn't stopped me, at that."

Duke lifted his head. "What the hell are you talking about?"

"Well, after that loudmouth come in here, that Donkey fella . . ."

"Donkey was here?"

"Sure, yesterday. She knew all about it and she said . . ."

Duke cut into the flow of words, "She? Who's she?"

"The gal. She's upstairs. Knew Donkey, knew all about the fuss in Holiday . . ."

Duke was already bounding up the steps, full of renewed life. "Maury! Maury, where are you? Maury!"

She opened the door to the room, standing there, looking at him, looking past him. "Duke! Where's Kitty?"

"Get on your riding clothes. Quick, damn it." He shoved her back into the room, grabbed her bag, began dragging out her possessions. "That skirt—you got it?"

"Duke, you mean you left her?"

"Didn't have a snowman's chance," he said. "Thought I might raise a posse here. O'Brien, Hoss, they're my friends from away back. No good, now. Get your clothes off!"

He found the divided skirt and thrust it at her. With fumbling hands she began to unbutton her clothes.

She asked, trembling, "Just you and me? Against them all? Duke—I can't."

He said, "They're bringing Judge Shelley out there to make it legal. You know what that means if they take Kitty?"

"I know, but . . ."

"I'm taking you there to make it goddam extra legal," he hammered at her. He turned his back as she mechanically began to undress. He saw the blue bottle on the dresser. He spun around, facing her.

He said, "There it is. The escape, the way out. You want to take it? Or do you want to go with me?"

She let the dress drop. She picked up the dark-blue riding skirt. She said humbly, "I guess I knew you'd come here and I knew I'd have to go with you. I'm scared. I'm blue scared to my toes. But I'll go."

Time, he thought now, how was the time element? The sun was westering. She could ride, at any rate. They could make a run for it. He tore down the stairs.

"Horses," he demanded of O'Brien. "Is there a fast horse I can get hold of?"

"I got me a pretty good one," said O'Brien. "And James Orr has got one down the street in the livery stable." He had a cartridge belt strung around his middle. He plucked a cane from a hook on the wall. "You know me, Duke. I ain't nothin' much. But what there is of me, you kept it goin'. Don't tell me I can't ride with you."

Duke said, "You can go along if you can keep up. Bring those horses around."

Maury came down in a minute. She looked lovely, he saw. Her shoulders had squared, and although she was pallid and the fear was in her, she had finally held to a decision. She asked, "Will we be in time, Duke?"

"In time for the funeral?" He laughed without humorous intent. "I don't know. There's a young fellow I'm sort of counting on. Maybe he can keep Kitty alive until we get there. Either way, Maury, there'll be a funeral."

Jack Budington had stopped struggling. He could not believe his eyes. It was a mockery, a joke. He said it so often that they threatened to gag him. Now he knew it was real; a filthy, rotten scene, the men looming, portentous, solemn, all of them against the pale girl standing at bay.

Possibly the trail boss was uneasy, but he stood like a clod, mouth hanging open a little. Poley Meyer and Soapy moved restlessly, but they had all gone too far to back down. Fairly had sent the rest of the men after the herd, and now Avidon's posse held the guns and the power and the glory.

It took longer than expected, and the sun was going down. Avidon had mapped out the town of Holiday with a stick, showing in the dust the way it was, the way Kitty had quarreled with Fitz Warren and had stabbed him. Avidon made it all sound reasonable in his southern voice and smooth way.

They had listened to Kitty, too. She told of Fitz's kindness, of losing the knife he had given her. She spoke of Maury, but had to admit Maury was gone. She admitted the argument with Fitz. She passionately denied the killing. But Duke was gone and Maury was gone, and it sounded weak, Jack Budington knew.

Nobody on the jury believed her—Jack could tell by the way they would not look at her when she was testifying. He cried out strongly, then, cursing them, and when Fairly told him to shut his mouth and behave, he fell into a kind of apathy.

Kitty fully realized what was happening. She could see the trees in the distance against the fading light. From one of those trees, she thought, that's where they'll hang me. They'll get rid of the trail drivers and then it will be dark, and they can do it much easier in the dark.

She heard Avidon going on and on. It was necessary to convince the trail men, she knew. The posse had already

condemned her, but the trail men would carry the story to
Dodge, up and down the length and breadth of the West,
wherever they drifted, and Avidon wanted it to be told his
way. He was painting her character as black as possible.
He was hinting at motives which confused her—she had
never taken anyone's money, she had never wanted to marry
Fitz for his money, it was ridiculous.

She laughed, and that was a mistake. They thought she was
hard, defiant when she uttered that crazy sound.

Jack Budington writhed, then. He sensed the bitter, lost,
hopeless weariness in her dry mirth. He shouted something
and again Fairly subdued him.

The judge was addressing the jury. "You will retire to a
place apart and in your good judgment and to the best of
your ability you will decide the guilt or innocence of this
accused person."

Then he went on. He had force, a dramatic gift. He
practically retried the case. He left no doubt in anyone's
mind of his own belief. He was twice as accusatory as
Avidon. His words bit at Kitty so that she shrank back,
confused, almost believing the man.

She sensed the venom in him, dimly recognized it as a
hatred of her, of all women. She had expected nothing from
him, but this was above and beyond the judge's duty. It was
her death knell, she thought.

The judge finished, the jury went self-consciously apart,
beyond hearing of the others. She heard Jack Budington
promising to kill Avidon, the judge, the jurors, one at a time,
whenever and wherever he found them. The words meant
nothing. By that time she would be moldering in a shallow
grave, or eaten by coyotes who would dig her up.

The jury came back very soon, before the sun had entirely
gone down behind the trees. She scarcely heard them.

"Guilty."

That was enough. She must have fainted, because rough
hands held her. They were taking away Jack Budington,
still bound with the reata, taking him back to the herd.
Fairly was telling him he was loco, that it was a true
trial, that Judge Shelley had the right, that Jack was better
off never to see her again, alive or dead.

They had gone, in haste to catch up with the herd, 'when
Shelley played his last part in the drama. By then the words
she had expected had lost meaning. "You shall be taken to
a place convenient to here and hanged by the neck until
dead, dead, dead."

How he loved to mouth the sentence, she thought as they

gathered around her. They tied her hands behind her, and she scarcely felt the pain of the rope.

Poley Meyer and Soapy Simms were protesting. The others yelled them down. It was a hullabaloo, but Poley and Soapy couldn't fight the whole posse. They got on their horses and rode away. They would not be a part of it, they made clear. Only the county sheriff had a right to hang a body, they said. But they rode away.

Rough hands put Kitty on a horse. She was scared. It was the funniest thing of all, how frightened she was to be on a horse. As if it made any difference.

Duke Parry cursed the descending sun. They had ridden the horses to foaming weariness. Then he saw the trail herd and spurred on. Maury and O'Brien were grimly behind. No one had spoken for an hour.

Jim, the segundo, told the story. Fairly and the others had not yet caught up. Duke begged for fresh horses, but the ones Maury and O'Brien were riding were no good for cutting or roping and Jim couldn't oblige, except to swap for the black.

They rode again. Maury was hunched in the saddle, fighting her fear, suffering every step of the way. O'Brien was stiff and sore. Duke drove them.

They saw figures, and Duke spurred his fresh mount. In the gathering dusk he recognized Fairly, saw Jack Budington under guard. He yanked the rifle from the boot, suspecting Fairly. He reined in yards away from the small party and demanded, "Where is Kitty?"

"They've got her condemned," Jack yelled. "I told these goddam fools they'd hang her."

Duke said, "If they haven't already."

"They'll hang her in due time," said Fairly. "The woman is guilty as sin. I heard the evidence."

"You're a stupid dam' idiot," said Duke. "I've got a witness, I've got proof the girl is innocent."

"You ran. I wouldn't believe you on a stack of Bibles," said Fairly. "Now get outa our way."

Duke lifted the muzzle of the rifle. "Turn Jack loose."

"I be damned if I do."

"You'll be dead if you don't."

O'Brien had caught up. Maury sat quietly, and the trail drivers stared curiously at her. O'Brien held his gun in his hand and said, "Duke's callin' the turn."

"You wouldn't dare start shootin'. Nobody's goin' to hang that gal. There's a judge and everything back there," Fairly argued. "They got the law there."

"You should be mixed up with such law," said Duke. "Cut Jack loose. I haven't got time to palaver."

Fairly hesitated. He was a brave man, but no gun fighter. He heared something in Duke's voice which was clear as the sound of a rattler.

He cut Jack loose. The young rancher came around and started southward without a word, knowing Duke would follow. Fairly looked after him, said, "The dumb clodhopper. We coulda had a spread as big as John Slaughter's."

Duke and his followers were already in motion. The sun ducked behind the last hill and the prairie became ghostly, silent except for the sound of pounding hoofs.

They had come to the trees. The rope was coiled in the hands of Sledge, who drooled a bit from the corners of his flaccid mouth. Yank, in the foreground with his drinking companion, suddenly fell back, stumbling a little in the dried leaves beneath the outstretched limb which Avidon had unerringly selected. Someone had constructed torches, and now they flared, illuminating the night.

Shelley's face was impassive; he had a firm grip on himself. Avidon sweated a little, his mouth closed tightly as if to keep the phlegm in his throat.

The light flickered on Kitty's face. Color had returned to her, she had regained the determination to make a good end. Someone said horsely, "She oughta have a hood over her. They always have a hood."

"A bandanna'll do," said Avidon. He came toward her.

She looked him in the face, but his eyes wavered, would not focus upon her. He had a dirty, sweated red kerchief in his hands. He made as if to tie it around her forehead, so that the folds would drape across her face.

She said with sudden strength, "No! If you can't watch me strangle, how can you hang me?"

Avidon said, "Hold still while I tie this."

She rolled and jerked her head, crying, "Cowards! You haven't got nerve enough to watch it. Filth! Scum!"

His attempts weakened. He could have forced the issue by manhandling her, but he was unable to do it, now, with death so close. He stood helpless, staring at Shelley.

The judge said tonelessly, "What difference? Proceed."

They chivvied the horse beneath the branch of the tree. Avidon threw the end of the rope up and over, brought it down. Sledge, grinning vacuously, had fashioned a hangman's noose with clumsy results. Avidon put it around her neck.

She felt the hard knot beneath her ear. Still she kept her head high, trying to look up, trying to keep her neck from canting to one side under the knot.

It was at least partially true about one's past life swimming by as the time neared. She saw her father quite plainly, his back bent, hauling the nets. She saw her brothers and sisters and then Fitz Warren, alive and kindly, also dead on the floor.

She said without volition, "As God is my witness, I did not kill Fitz. I truly believe he was murdered by Simon Avidon and Donkey. These are my dying words: I am innocent."

Yank whimpered something. The others stood firm, committed, unable to stir. Sledge was still grinning, he himself could not have told why. Shelley was stick-straight, standing close to Avidon.

A man said, "For Chrissake, get it over with."

It was then that Duke rode out of the darkness.

They had come in quietly, despite Jack Budington's half-insane pleas for a sudden volley which would kill half the posse straight off. The girl was on the horse, the rope around her neck, Duke pointed out. A burst of action could cause her to be jerked into eternity.

Jack had suffered, but accepted the stark necessity of silence and care. O'Brien was shaky, but the sight of Kitty with the rope around her neck nerved him. Maury fought with the impulse to vomit, stayed close to Duke. The two men remained outside the light of the torches while she and Duke rode in.

They could not win. There were too many dedicated to the deed. Duke held his rifle under his left arm, his revolver in his right hand. The reins were loose on the pony's neck as he kneed the animal in and said in cold, loud accents, "Who wants it first?"

The hard fact of his drawn and ready weapons gave him a moment or two. It was all he could hope for, and he took advantage of it. "I've got new evidence. I demand this kangaroo court be reopened right now."

Avidon said, "The woman's been tried and convicted."

"New evidence, I said." He nodded toward the judge, always watching Avidon's guns. "You hear me, Judge Shelley?"

"The court has spoken. I don't acknowledge any such evidence."

Avidon insisted, "You're buckin' the law. This party is legal, and the woman is guilty."

"How many of you want to stand on that? I've got a witness, Maury Dent. I've got guns out yonder covering y'all. How many want to die on the word of Avidon and the judge?" Duke demanded.

He knew they were caught up in their determination to hang Kitty, that there was no way for them to back down. He wanted time, he wanted to find a way to do this without killing and without himself and O'Brien and Maury and Jack dying.

Judge Shelley said, "I've pronounced sentence. There is no appeal."

"Anyone interfering here will be an outlaw," shouted Avidon. "I'll hunt them down with dogs!"

"You won't be alive." Duke moved hs gun muzzles. "You nor the judge nor a few others."

"He can't pull it out," said Avidon to the posse. "You heard him, men. He's said he'd kill us."

The man had a certain nerve, thought Duke. Maybe he was counting on the uncertain light, the fact that Duke could not be completely accurate from the saddle—counting on his luck, Shelley, his idea of the law upholding him. At any rate, it was going to be tough.

He said again, "All I want's a new hearing. Maury can prove Kitty lost the knife, didn't have it when Fitz was stabbed."

"That's a dam' lie!" The first note of panic was in Avidon's voice. He flicked a glance at Shelley.

"Lies," agreed the judge. "The law has taken its course. You stand in contempt, Duke Parry."

"Nobody could have more contempt for this court than I have," said the Duke. "All right. Put up or shut up. Make your play. Let's all die right here, if that's your idea of the law."

He might have made it, at that. The posse was at a standstill in its thinking. The fervor of the lynching had felt the cold touch of reason. Duke's appeal for a new trial might have swayed enough of them.

It was Sledge, the panting dimwit, who set it off. He slapped the flank of the horse on which Kitty was sitting.

The horse bolted. Kitty hung suspended from the end of the rope, spinning in the flickering light of the torches. Nothing could hold Jack Budington then. He came in shooting, aiming his pony's head for the tree.

Duke dropped from the saddle, yelling at Maury to do

the same. O'Brien fired a shot and a posseman swore, clutching at his shoulder, going down in the dirt.

Duke's feet rustled on the leaves as he moved. Shelley produced a derringer.

There was no sight of Avidon. The posse had begun to throw bullets. Duke's horse screamed and bolted as lead struck it.

He could not see Kitty and Jack. He fired the rifle several times. It wasn't any good. A torch had dropped to earth and was flickering. If it went out, the poorest shot was his equal.

There were too many guns, he thought. O'Brien was staying out and trying to pick them off, but the little gambler had never been a great marksman and the light was too bad. Jack must be occupied with Kitty, whether or not she had broken her neck.

He got a glimpse of Sledge. He fired once. He moved and lined up the milling crowd. Bullets cut around him. It wouldn't be long before they found lodging in his body.

He saw Shelley. The judge was aiming in the direction of Jack and the girl, Duke knew. That would be the judge, all right.

He stepped past a rearing horse and said softly, "Judge, here it is."

He killed Shelley without a thought. He was intent on Avidon, seeking him in the shrieking, howling melee. He found Jack and Kitty, saw the young rancher riding out with the girl in his arms. He saw Shelley writhing on the ground, holding his middle, and the sight comforted him and steadied him.

Half of their stinking law, he thought. Now, if I could only smoke out the marshal.

Sledge had a rifle and was spraying it around, dancing and frothing at the mouth. He stepped into the half-light, and Duke picked him off with a careless shot. Sledge fell across the flame, his clothes smoldered, then burned a little.

Avidon was coming. He had his gun leveled, and his face was contorted. He had seen Shelley die and his world collapse and all the fruits of his years in Holiday drop from the trees.

Duke swerved, letting the first shot go by him. Then he went forward.

They came together, Duke's left hand striking, snakelike. Duke's pistol shoved into the belly of the marshal. He deflected Avidon's aim with his shrewd blow.

He pulled the trigger, thumbed it, pulled it again and again. Then the gun was empty. He drew back and slugged

124   William R. Cox

at the head of the man as he fell, knowing he was killing
a dead man, not caring, his rage utterly controlling him.

There were two shots spaced, there was a yell. Duke let
the body fall, pulled away, thumbing cartridges into the
chambers of the pistol. He heard voices which were familiar.

Poley Meyer was saying at the top of his lungs, "Put up
your hawglegs. Light them torches. Settle down, or we'll cut
down every mother's son of you."

Soapy Simms was with him. They sat their horses, com-
manding the stricken field. There was no voice of authority
left to the posse. Silence fell like a blanket.

Duke rolled Sledge's body aside, picked up the brand,
shook it to full blaze. He said, "Glad to see you along,
Poley."

"We was too far away at the beginnin'," said Poley
apologetically. "Had a notion you'd be back. Augured about
it some. Then we started back. Couldn't stomach hangin'
her, after all."

Duke said, "What we need is a burying detail."

He felt worn and weary. He hadn't had enough sleep. He
had ridden in the drag, he had pounded the road and the
trail, he was all of a sudden worn out.

Avidon's clothing was afire from the shots poured in at
close range. Poley came and stared, then stomped out the
blaze. "Reckon I'd better take the torch. Reckon I'd better
take charge, me and Soapy, somehow."

"Yeah. You do that," said Duke. He started to turn away,
his mind blank. Too many men had died for the law of
Avidon and Shelley.

Someone replenished the other torches. Duke stumbled
in the reflected light. He felt a soft hand in his, looked at
Maury without recognition, then started. He had forgotten
all about her.

She said, "I didn't run, Duke. I was there all the time."

"Kitty?" His mind was reorganizing. "Jack?"

"Over here."

Kitty was stretched on the ground, her head in the lap of
the young rancher. He was crooning to her. What he said
didn't make sense, it was also none of anybody's business.
Kitty's neck was burned by the rope, but she was alive.
She was smiling up at Jack and hoarsely repeating the things
he was saying to her. It made a sort of croaking chorus. Like
frogs, Duke thought confusedly.

He turned away. "Didn't break her fool neck, anyway."

Maury said, "I didn't even want to run. You were in it,
and I got down behind the horse and wished I had a gun."

The light was good to her. She shone; not only her bright eyes, but everything about her shone. He had always known she could be a hell of a woman.

"I wished I had the blue bottle, so I could smash it. I wished you'd care that I wanted to do that and then die when you died."

He said, "Now, wait." Things clicked into place. It was an effort. He had never been a man for killing unless it was more than necessary. The manner in which he had destroyed Avidon had left him shaken to the core. "We've got to do certain things. Another trial. You'll have to testify. There'll be a new judge, lawyers, everything. Kitty'll have to go in."

"Yes, Duke. Tomorrow, some other time."

They were looking over the dead and wounded. Old Poley Meyer and Soapy were getting things under control. Yank had reappeared and was acting as their underling. After all, thought Duke, the riff raff that comprised the posse deserved no more than it got.

He said, "Reckon Jack's cattle will get to Dodge without him, all right. Reckon there's nothing more to do here."

"What do you mean?" she asked softly.

"O'Brien?" he called.

"Been stayin' out of it," said the quiet voice from the nearby shadows. "Don't figure they know I'm around. Like to keep it that way, if you don't mind."

"I'll get me a horse," said Duke. "Have a word with Poley. You wait here."

He went back to the scene of the fight. He said to Poley, "I'm a bit weary. Holiday is no place for me right now. Relatives and friends might get excited. Maybe Kitty ought to be taken to Red River, you think?"

Poley said, "Hell, I'm actin' marshal on my own say-so. What if I deputize you?"

Duke said, "That'll do it. Send for us when it's time."

"Glad to handle it thataway," said Poley. He added, "Time there was a new deal in Holiday."

"I'll buy a stack," said Duke.

When he turned, Maury was still beside him. They found horses which dead men would not need. They sent O'Brien to give the glad news to Jack and Kitty.

Then they mounted and rode northward, the five of them. Maury hummed a tune to herself—she had an excellent voice. The moon came out. Duke looked at her from time to time.

She looked fine. The turmoil began to die within him. He wasn't a marrying man, but Maury sure looked fine for now.

Kitty and Jack Budington looked only at each other. Well, there was a preacher in Red River Station. Kitty had a right. She had fully earned it.

In the end, he thought with new cheer, everybody's honor would be satisfied.

William R. Cox was born in Peapack, New Jersey. His early career was in newspaper journalism. In the late 1930s he began writing sports, crime, and adventure stories for the magazine market, and he made his debut as a Western writer with "Night of the Blood Bucket Raid" in *Dime Western* in the January, 1941 issue. It is worth noting that his Western story debut was with the first of several stories to feature a series character, Terry Glenn. During the 1940s Cox created a number of other series characters for the magazine market, most notably the Whistler Kid who appeared regularly in *10 Story Western* and Duke Bagley whose adventures usually were featured in *Star Western*. "The short story form was blissful until there were no markets," he once recalled. In the 1950s and 1960s Cox turned to television and wrote at least a hundred teleplays for such series as "Broken Arrow," "Dick Powell's Zane Grey Theater," "The Virginian," and "Bonanza." He also won a host of readers writing original paperback Western novels, the best known of which are novels about the adventures of two series characters originally published by Fawcett Gold Medal: Cemetery Jones in a series published under his own byline and the Tom Buchanan series which appeared under the house name, Jonas Ward. Dale L. Walker in the second edition of *Twentieth Century Western Writers* (1991) commented that William R. Cox's Western "novels are noted for their 'page-turner' pace, realistic dialogue, and frequent Colt-and-Winchester gun play. The series of novels built around the strong West Texas character, Tom Buchanan, are very typical Cox Western." Among his non-series Western novels, his most notable titles are *Comanche Moon* (1959), *The Gunsharp* (1965), and *Moon at Cobre* (1969).